全書外師親錄MP3音檔

（因手機系統不同，音檔建議直接下載至電腦，
下載方式詳見封底折口）

70篇精選會話╳關鍵文法句型，
更揪出常見文法錯誤，

從日常會話開始，再進入職場，
每天一單元，道地英文現學現説！
想要加入外商，這一本通通幫你搞定！

前進外商 **第1步**

從日常生活到職場會話,開口說英文不用怕

本書精選70篇日常生活及職場會話,並附有專業外師的親錄音檔,幫助讀者在生活、在職場都能夠開口說英文!

01 你看起來不對勁

情境對話 ∩ Track 01

看見朋友身體不舒服,自己卻難以提供協助,只能給予言語上的關心,並督促朋友多多休息,早日去看醫生。

A: You don't look too good. Are you OK?
你看起來不大對勁。你還好嗎?

B: No, I'm not OK. My head is pounding. I feel like throwing up.
不,我不好。我的頭好痛。我想吐。

A: Oh, no. Have you seen a doctor?
噢,真糟。你看過醫生了嗎?

B: No. I'll just have some painkillers and lie down for a while.
還沒。我吃點止痛藥然後躺一下就好了。

A: But you need to go to see a doctor. You look pale!
可是你必須去看醫生才行。你看起來好蒼白!

B: That's all right. I just need some rest. I haven't slept three nights in a row.
沒關係,我休息一下就好。我已經連續三個晚上沒睡覺了。

A: Don't work like a horse. Take good care of yourself.
別那麼拼命工作了。好好照顧自己。

B: Thank you. I will.
謝謝。我會的。

關鍵單字要認得

pound
動 猛擊、敲打

I could feel my heart pounding as I met my wife first time.
→ 第一次見到我的妻子時,我可以感覺到心臟在狂跳。

012

前進外商 **第2步**

打好基礎,學會關鍵單字與片語

本書每篇情境對話都整理出關鍵單字及片語,也附上延伸例句供讀者參考,讓讀者可以更深入理解文意,也能夠學到更多!

row up 嘔吐	**He threw up all over his clothes yesterday.** → 他昨天吐得整件衣服都是。
ainkiller 止痛藥	**I will have some painkillers for my headache.** → 我會吃一些止痛藥來治好的頭痛。
e down 躺下	**The teacher asked him to lie down for a while.** → 老師要他躺下來一會兒。
ale 蒼白的	**David was pale with fear.** → 大衛害怕到臉色發白。
n a row 連續	**He could not sleep three nights in a row.** → 他連續三個晚上沒辦法睡覺。

一定要會的萬用句

- You don't look too good. → 你看起來不大對勁。
- I feel like throwing up. → 我想吐。
- You look pale! → 你看起來好蒼白！
- I just need some rest. → 我休息一下就好。

我們也能這樣說

1 You look dreadful. → 你看起來很糟。
2 My nose is clogged. I can't breathe.
→ 我的鼻子塞住了，不能呼吸。
3 She has a migraine. → 她偏頭痛。
4 I am better now. → 我現在好多了。
5 Your resistance is down. → 你的抵抗力變差了。

013

前進外商 **第3步**

不只學好萬用句，
也能夠換句話說

每篇情境對話還有加碼補充延
伸例句，讓同一情境中可以選
用的句子大幅增加，無論什麼
話題都不用擔心詞窮！

常見錯誤不要犯

在說一個人臉色看起來很不好的時候，可能會下意識脫口而出 "You don't look too health." 但這句話是錯的！

正確的說法是 "You don't look too good."

look 是連綴動詞，後面都是接形容詞，所以這個句子中應用形容詞 good 而不是名詞 health。其他連綴動詞還有：taste / sound / feel / smell。

常見句型 一起學

★ 完成式疑問句

Have you seen a doctor ?

Have + 主詞 + 過去分詞 + 受詞 +（其他補語）

完成式疑問句，用來詢問別人某件事是否做過了，這個句型強調「已經……了嗎？」這種感覺，重點是要記得使用 "have" 以及動詞要改為過去分詞。

以下是其他的相關例句：

▶ **Have you had breakfast yet ?**
→ 你吃早餐了嗎？
▶ **Have I passed the exam?**
→ 我通過考試了嗎？
▶ **Has he told her the truth?**
→ 他跟她說實話了嗎？
▶ **Has she been to the U.S.?**
→ 她曾去過美國嗎？
▶ **Have they worked here before?**
→ 他們以前在這裡工作過嗎？
▶ **Have they watched the movie?**
→ 他們看過電影了嗎？

014

前進外商 **第4步**

常見錯誤不要犯，
常見句型一起學

本書另外點出常見的文法錯誤，
提醒讀者小心盲點，也詳細解析
會話中出現的句型，補充相關文
法知識，讓讀者全方位學英文！

在全球化的現在，進入跨國公司工作不只能開闊視野，更能提升薪資待遇，若有機會就該把握！但機會是給準備好的人，想進入外商，除了要了解公司的主力產品、背景和歷史，並釐清工作職責外，外語能力當然也是要精進的。

需要的外語能力不只是商務英語，平時的日常會話也不能輕忽。日常會話是在國外生活的必要能力，也能讓你與公司的同事、國外的客戶建立更親密的關係。在前進外商前，得先掌握日常會話，再來開始鑽研商務英語。

商務英語包含公司內部的公事交流、訂單的確認、與客戶的聯絡等，當然，工作績效、產品的優惠活動等也是包含其中。在外商工作時，要能夠見招拆招，即時反應。

希望進入外商工作的人之中，有些雖然英文讀寫能力很強，卻苦於「不敢說」，害怕發音不標準，或是害怕文法不小心用錯，而不敢在外國人面前大方說英文。但這樣不是很可惜嗎？不只實力無法發揮，還錯失了前進外商的機會！

要克服「不敢說」的困境，可以從簡單的會話開始學習，一步一步習慣說英語，並建立自信心，久而久之自然就能把英文說得越來越溜了！

因此，這本書中精選「閒話家常」及「公事公辦」兩個部分，分別是日常生活及職場會用到的情境會話，從日常生活開始，用較沒有壓力的會話來培養「開口說」的自信心。熟悉了之後，再進一步加強難度，練習職場會話，為進入外商做準備。本書的所有會話都特別聘請外師親錄，讓讀者可以跟著外師一句一句念，習慣英文會話的節奏與說話方式。

為了幫助讀者能更快適應開口說英文，本書除了會話之外，也特別整理出「關鍵單字」、「萬用句」、「換句話說」等內容，讓讀者能迅速掌握常用句，迅速建立起一套自己習慣的英文表達方式。

「常見錯誤不要犯」、「常見句型一起學」也是本書的重點，前者幫助讀者找出自己盲點並糾正才能免於貽笑大方，後者拆解常用的句型，讓讀者熟悉文法概念，也能再自行換句話說、舉一反三，打好英文基礎。

想要前進外商，不能不會英文，如果經過多方考量還是決定不進入外商，英文能力也仍舊在職場上是一個利器，能帶來更多的升遷機會。希望本書能幫助讀者從簡單的會話開始，一步步培養英文開口說的自信心與口說能力！

Kevin Zhu

許澄瑄

Part1 閒話家常

Part2 公事公辦

Part 1
閒話家常

01 你看起來不對勁

看見好友身體不舒服，自己卻難以提供協助，只能給予言語上的關心，並督促朋友多多休息，早日去看醫生。

A: You don't look too good. Are you OK?	你看起來不大對勁。你還好嗎？
B: No, I'm not OK. My head is pounding. I feel like throwing up.	不，我不好。我的頭好痛。我想吐。
A: Oh, no. Have you seen a doctor?	噢，真糟。你看過醫生了嗎？
B: No. I'll just have some painkillers and lie down for a while.	還沒。我吃點止痛藥然後躺一下就好了。
A: But you need to go to see a doctor. You look pale!	可是你必須去看醫生才行。你看起來好蒼白！
B: That's all right. I just need some rest. I haven't slept three nights in a row.	沒關係，我休息一下就好。我已經連續三個晚上沒睡覺了。
A: Don't work like a horse. Take good care of yourself.	別那麼拼命工作了。好好照顧自己。
B: Thank you. I will.	謝謝。我會的。

 關鍵單字要認得

pound
☑ 猛擊、敲打

I could feel my heart pounding as I met my wife first time.
→ 第一次見到我的妻子時，我可以感覺到心臟在狂跳。

throw up
ph. 嘔吐

He threw up all over his clothes yesterday.
→ 他昨天吐得整件衣服都是。

painkiller
n. 止痛藥

I will have some painkillers for my headache.
→ 我會吃一些止痛藥來治我的頭痛。

lie down
ph. 躺下

The teacher asked him to lie down for a while.
→ 老師要他躺下來一會兒。

pale
adj. 蒼白的

David was pale with fear.
→ 大衛害怕到臉色發白。

in a row
ph. 連續

He could not sleep three nights in a row.
→ 他連續三個晚上沒辦法睡覺。

 一定要會的萬用句

1 You don't look too good. → 你看起來不大對勁。

2 I feel like throwing up. → 我想吐。

3 You look pale! → 你看起來好蒼白！

4 I just need some rest. → 我休息一下就好。

我們也能這樣說

1 You look dreadful. → 你看起來很糟。

2 My nose is clogged. I can't breathe.

→ 我的鼻子塞住了，不能呼吸。

3 She has a migraine. → 她偏頭痛。

4 I am better now. → 我現在好多了。

5 Your resistance is down. → 你的抵抗力變差了。

常見錯誤不要犯

在說一個人臉色看起來很不好的時候，可能會下意識脫口而出 "You don't look too health." 但這句話是錯的！

正確的說法是 "You don't look too good."

look 是連綴動詞，後面都是接形容詞。所以這個句子中應用形容詞 good 而不是名詞 health。其他連綴動詞還有：taste / sound / feel / smell。

常見句型一起學

★ 完成式疑問句

Have you seen a doctor ?

Have ＋ 主詞 ＋ 過去分詞 ＋ 受詞 ＋（其他補語）

完成式疑問句，用來詢問別人某件事是否做過了，這個句型強調「已經……了嗎？」這種感覺，重點是要記得使用 "have" 以及動詞要改為過去分詞。

以下是其他的相關例句：

▶ **Have you had breakfast yet ?**
→ 你吃早餐了嗎？

▶ **Have I passed the exam?**
→ 我通過考試了嗎？

▶ **Has he told her the truth?**
→ 他跟她說實話了嗎？

▶ **Has she been to the U.S.?**
→ 她曾去過美國嗎？

▶ **Have they worked here before?**
→ 他們以前在這裡工作過嗎？

▶ **Have they watched the movie?**
→ 他們看過電影了嗎？

02 她看起來非常美麗

看到喜歡的影集或電影，總會忍不住和人分享心得，在分享心得之餘，也可能會再聊到自己的生活。

A: Fanny looks gorgeous. She's the most beautiful bride on TV shows I've ever seen.	芬妮看起來美極了。她是我見過電視劇中最美麗的新娘。
B: Yeah, she looks stunning.	對啊，她美呆了。
A: I love her wedding gown. I want my wedding dress to look like that.	我好喜歡她的婚紗。我的婚紗也要像她的一樣
B: It totally looks good on her.	她穿起來真的很好看。
A: Oh, I wish I could get married soon, too. Ah, will my boyfriend ever propose to me?	噢，我也好想趕快結婚喔。啊，我男友到底會不會跟我求婚呢？
B: You can pop the question to him instead!	妳可以反過來跟他求婚啊。
A: I can't do that!	不可以啦！
B: Why not? Girl also has the right to propose. Equality between men and women.	為什麼不可以呢？女孩子也有權利求婚啊。男女平等嘛。

 關鍵單字要認得

gorgeous
adj. 極美的

My wife is so gorgeous that my heart was pounding as I met her first time. → 我的妻子太美了，所以第一次見到她時，我的心臟在狂跳。

stunning *adj.* 非常美麗的	**Amy looks stunning in the red dress.** → 穿那件紅裙子的艾咪非常美麗。
gown *n.* 禮服、長袍	**She needs a gown for the wedding.** → 她需要為婚禮準備禮服。
get married *ph.* 結婚	**He got married last year.** → 他去年結婚了。
propose to *ph.* 向某人求婚	**He proposed to his girlfriend yesterday.** → 他昨天向他的女友求婚了。
pop the question *ph.* 求婚	**She decided to pop the question to her boyfriend.** → 她決定向她的男友求婚。

- -

 一定要會的萬用句

① She looks stunning. → 她美呆了。

② It totally looks good on her. → 她穿起來真的很好看。

③ You can pop the question to him instead!

→ 妳可以反過來跟他求婚啊！

④ Equality between men and women. → 男女平等。

 我們也能這樣說

① To the man who has conquered the bride's heart.

→ 恭喜新郎擄獲新娘的心。

② I'd like to make a toast. → 我想舉杯說幾句祝賀的話。

③ She looks lovely in that wedding gown. → 她穿那件婚紗真好看。

④ May she share everything with her husband, including the housework. → 希望新郎、新娘分享一切，包括做家事。

常見錯誤不要犯

在說到求婚時,不熟英文的人可能認為求婚的片語中有個the question,所以 "You can ask the question to him." 也可以說是求婚,但這句話是錯的!

正確的說法是 "You can pop the question to him!"

ask the question 意為「問問題」;pop the question 意為「求婚」。表達求婚還可以說:propose marriage, propose to 等。

常見句型一起學

★「最高級」後接「that 子句」

She is the most beautiful bride on TV shows

主詞 + be 動詞　　　+ 補語(最高級＋名詞)

(that) I've ever seen.

＋　　　　that 子句

在這個句型中,一定要使用「最高級」;後接「that 子句」,不過「that」這個關係代名詞通常可以省略。

以下是其他的相關例句:

▶ **He is the cutest guy I've ever known.**
→ 他是我所認識的人當中最帥的男生。

▶ **We are the best varsity team our school ever had.**
→ 我們是學校有史以來最強的校隊。

▶ **She is probably the most irresponsible mother ever.**
→ 她可能是有史以來最不負責任的媽媽!

▶ **They are the sweetest students I've ever had.**
→ 他們是我教過最貼心的學生。

03 問你一個私人問題

即使交的是網友，只要是朋友，就會忍不住關心對方生活大小事，可能會問出和他人隱私相關的問題，這種時候用詞就要更小心了。

A: Can I ask you a personal question?	我可以問你一個私人問題嗎？
B: Sure, go ahead. What do you want to know?	可以啊，妳問吧。妳想知道什麼？
A: Uh, are you and Jolie seeing each other?	呃，你和裘莉在交往嗎？
B: What? Of course not! Who told you that?	什麼？當然沒有！誰告訴妳的？
A: A little bird told me that you two are living in the same apartment.	有人偷偷跟我說你們兩個住在同一間公寓裡。
B: We are, but that's because we are relatives. She's my cousin!	我們是住在一起，但那是因為我們是親戚。她是我堂妹！
A: So that's the way it is. I am sorry. I misunderstood.	原來是這樣。抱歉哦，我誤會了。
B: It doesn't matter. Forget it.	沒關係。算了。

 關鍵單字要認得

personal *adj.* 私人的、個人的	**I will take all my personal belongings with me when I leave.** → 我離開的時候會帶走所有個人物品。

seeing each other *ph.* 在交往	**Amy and my brother are seeing each other.** → 艾咪和我哥哥正在交往。
of course not *ph.* 當然沒有	**Of course not! I didn't win the game.** → 當然不！我沒有贏得那盤遊戲。
a little bird told me *ph.* 有人私下告訴我、我聽說	**A little bird told me that John didn't pass the test.** → 有人私下告訴我約翰沒有通過考試。
apartment *n.* 公寓	**I live in the apartment near the school.** → 我住在學校附近的公寓裡。
relative *n.* 親戚	**He doesn't live with any relatives after moving to another city.** → 搬去另一個城市後，他沒有再和任何親戚同住。

- -

 一定要會的萬用句

❶ Can I ask you a personal question? → 我可以問你一個私人問題嗎？

❷ Are you and Jolie seeing each other? → 你和裘莉在交往嗎？

❸ A little bird told me. → 我聽說的。

❹ I misunderstood. → 我誤會了。

我們也能這樣說

❶ Can I ask you something? → 我可以問你一件事嗎？

❷ Shoot! → 說吧！

❸ Good question. → 問得好。

❹ You got me there. → 你問倒我了。

❺ Let me put it this way. → 我這樣說好了。

常見錯誤不要犯

在説到交往時，不熟英文的人可能認為交往的片語中有和對方見面的
涵義在，所以 "Are you and Jolie meeting each other?" 也可以説是交
往，但這句話是錯的！

正確的説法是 "Are you and Jolie seeing each other?"

meet each other 意為「相遇」；而 see each other 有「約會、交往、
戀愛」的意思。雖然表面上看，see 和 meet 意思差不多，但兩個片語
表達的意思卻完全不同。

常見句型一起學

★ 實用疑問句

What　　do　　you　want　to　　　know ?

疑問詞　+　助動詞　+　主詞　+　want　+　不定詞 +（其他補語）

這個疑問句型非常實用，用來詢問對方想要做什麼事，可以立刻得到需要的資訊，
是一定要熟記的日常句型。

以下是其他的相關例句：

▶ **What do you want to eat?**
→ 你想吃什麼？

▶ **What does he want to buy?**
→ 他想買什麼？

▶ **What does she want to do?**
→ 她想做什麼？

▶ **What do they want to drink?**
→ 他們想喝什麼？

▶ **What do we want to achieve?**
→ 我們想達成什麼？

04 誰會贏得比賽

 **情境對話** ∩ **Track 04**

和朋友聊天的時候，可能相談甚歡，也可能意見不合，這種時候要控制好自己的語氣，不要真的吵起架來喔。

A: Who do you think will win this game?	你覺得這場比賽誰會贏？
B: Well, I'm in favor of the Yankees. They've had a good season.	嗯，我覺得洋基隊會贏。他們這一季表現得很搶眼。
A: Sorry to interrupt, but Red Sox will take this one hands down.	抱歉打斷你講話，不過紅襪隊一定能輕易贏得這場比賽。
B: No way. They've had a bad season so far.	不可能。他們這季到目前為止表現得很差。
A: No. Yankees won't win. They suck.	不。洋基隊不會贏的。他們打得很爛。
B: 30 bucks say you're wrong!	我賭三十美元，賭你都錯了。
A: OK. but I'd rather bet you $50 that you are wrong!	好。不過我寧願賭五十美元，賭你錯了。
B: Fine. Deal!	好的。一言為定！

 關鍵單字要認得

in favor of
ph. 支持、贊成

Sam is in favor of May's proposal.
→ 山姆支持梅的提案。

season
n. 球季、季節

There are four seasons in a year.
→ 一年有四個季節。

interrupt
v. 打斷

Please don't interrupt when others are talking.
→ 別人在說話的時候請不要出言打斷。

hands down
ph. 輕而易舉地

I will win the game hands down.
→ 我會輕而易舉地贏得遊戲。

so far
ph. 到目前為止

I didn't see anybody so far.
→ 目前為止，我沒有看到任何人。

buck
n. 一美元（口語）

I bet 50 bucks that she forgets the test.
→ 我賭50美元她忘了考試。

 一定要會的萬用句

1 I'm in favor of the Yankees. → 我覺得洋基隊會贏。

2 They've had a good season. → 他們這一季表現得很搶眼。

3 They suck. → 他們打得很爛。

4 Deal! → 一言為定！

 我們也能這樣說

1 Who do you think will get a perfect score on this test?
→ 你覺得這次考試誰會拿滿分？

2 I think our class leader will easily get a high score.
→ 我覺得我們班長能輕易拿下高分。

3 Do you mind if I cut in? → 介意我插個話嗎？

4 I agree with you there. → 我同意你的看法。

5 Please don't keep interrupting our conversation.
→ 請不要一直打斷我們的談話。

常見錯誤不要犯

在説到一個人或一支隊伍很糟糕的時候，最直覺的説法會是"They are bad."
這句話沒有不對，但絕對有更好的説法。

更好的説法是"They suck."

bad 這個形容詞過於普通。而 suck 這個詞在口語當中非常常用，
是俚語「糟糕的」的意思。例如：This football team really sucks.
這個足球隊真遜。

常見句型一起學

★ 實用疑問句

Who   **do you think**   **will**   **win**   **this**   **game** ?

疑問詞 +   插入句   +助動詞 + 動詞 + （受詞）+（其他補語）

這是個詢問他人意見的實用句型，留意插入句「do you think」的位置。

以下是其他的相關例句：

▶ **Who do you think will take part in the competition?**
→ 你覺得誰會參加競賽？

▶ **Who do you think will turn out to be a better man?**
→ 你覺得誰會是更好的男人？

▶ **Who do you think will run the marathon?**
→ 你覺得誰會參加馬拉松？

▶ **Who do you think will be elected this year?**
→ 你覺得今年誰會當選？

▶ **Who do you think will perform in the play?**
→ 你覺得誰會在這部戲劇裡演出？

05 你看起來美極了

只要是交友，對方也可能會來問你的意見，這些意見不限於談心、購物等生活瑣事，也可能會聊到彼此的外貌，這時候要好好稱讚、鼓勵對方喔。

A: You look good. Do you have a date?	你看起來很漂亮。你要去約會嗎？
B: Yes. Be honest with me, how do I look?	是的，老實跟我說，我看起來如何？
A: You look gorgeous. Nice skirt. You should wear skirts more often.	妳看起來美極了。很好看的裙子。妳應該要多穿裙子才對。
B: You really think so? I always thought I had chubby ankles.	你真的這樣覺得嗎？我一直覺得我的腳踝肥肥的。
A: No, your legs are straight, aren't they? You should be more confident.	哪有，妳的腿很直，不是嗎？妳應該要更有自信一點。
B: Thank you. You look good, too.	謝謝你。你也很好看。

關鍵單字要認得

honest
adj. 老實的、誠實的

I'm always honest with you.
→ 我對你一直都很誠實。

skirt
n. 裙子

She looks stunning in the blue skirt.
→ 她穿那條藍裙子很漂亮。

straight *adj.* 筆直的	**Go straight along this road and you will see the convenient store.** → 這條路直走，然後你就會看到便利商店。
confident *adj.* 自信的	**He didn't sound confident about the test.** → 聽起來他對考試沒有信心。

. . . .

 一定要會的萬用句

❶ How do I look?

→ 我看起來如何？

❷ You look gorgeous.

→ 你看起來美極了。

❸ You really think so?

→ 你真的這樣覺得嗎？

❹ You should be more confident.

→ 你應該要更有自信一點。

 我們也能這樣說

❶ This dress is so tight. I think I'll have to take it off.

→ 這件洋裝太緊了，我想還是脫掉好了。

❷ No, you look stunning in it.

→ 不會啊，妳穿這件看起來好迷人喔。

❸ What do you think? Don't you think she's beautiful?

→ 你覺得呢？你不覺得她很美嗎？

❹ Don't try to sweet talk me.

→ 別對我甜言蜜語。

❺ I mean it. → 我是說真的。

常見錯誤不要犯

想稱讚一個人很漂亮的時候，最直覺的說法會是"You look pretty."
這句話沒有不對，但絕對有更好的說法。

更好的說法是 "You look gorgeous."

You look pretty. 同樣也是「你很美／你很漂亮」的意思，但是表達上
就顯得過於普通，稱讚的程度也不強烈。 gorgeous 意為「華麗的、
燦爛的、好極了」。表示誇讚的程度更深。

常見句型一起學

★ 原本一直以為……

I   always   thought   I had chubby ankles.

主詞 + 頻率副詞 + 動詞過去式 +   子句（過去式）

主要句子與子句都是過去式，並搭配頻率副詞「always」，用來表示「原本一直以
為……」，但事實卻不一定跟所想的一致。

以下是其他的相關例句：

▶ **I always thought I was a creative person.**
→ 我一直以為我是個有創意的人。

▶ **I always thought he was a cheater.**
→ 我一直以為他是個騙子。

▶ **She always thought I was a man of my words.**
→ 她一直以為我是個守信用的人。

▶ **We always thought they were college students.**
→ 我們一直以為他們是大學生。

▶ **You always thought she was a kind-hearted woman.**
→ 你一直以為她是個好心腸的女人。

06 什麼事讓你煩惱

 情境對話　∩ Track 06

和朋友聊天的時候，對方可能會心情非常不好，這時候就需要你的安慰，也可以試著幫他找出解決事情的方法，即使不在彼此身邊，也能成為對方的助力。

A: You don't look good. What's bothering you?	你看起來不太好。什麼事讓你煩惱？
B: I'll never finish my assignment by today!	我今天一定無法完成我被交代的事！
A: Why don't you ask for an extension?	你為什麼不要求延長時間呢？
B: I don't think It's gonna work. Ms. Brown won't agree. She totally hates me!	沒有用的啦！布朗小姐不會同意的。她真的很討厭我！
A: No, she doesn't hate you. Just go talk to her. You never know.	她才不討厭你。你就去跟她談談嘛。不試試怎麼知道不行呢？
B: Yeah, I think you're right. OK. I'll call her right now.	是啊，我想妳說得對。好吧，我現在就打電話給她。
A: Good for you and good luck.	做得好，祝你好運。

 關鍵單字要認得

assignment
ｎ 作業、任務

I ask him to finish his assignment in two hours.
→ 我要求他在兩小時內完成他的作業。

ask for *ph.* 要求	**She couldn't ask for a better teacher.** → 她不能再找到更好的老師了。
extension *n.* 延期、延長	**I hope to get an extension of my assignment.** → 我希望作業的繳交期限能夠延長。
agree *v.* 同意	**John agreed with Amy on this issue.** → 約翰在這個議題上同意艾咪的意見。
right now *ph.* 立刻、馬上	**You'd better apologize right now.** → 你最好馬上道歉。

• •

 一定要會的萬用句

❶ What's bothering you? → 什麼事讓你煩惱？

❷ Why don't you ask for an extension?

→ 你為什麼不要求延長時間呢？

❸ I don't think it's gonna work. → 沒有用的啦。

❹ You never know. → 不試試怎麼知道不行呢？

 我們也能這樣說

❶ How do you find the information quickly? → 你是如何快速找到資料的？

❷ I need more time to find information on the Internet.

→ 我需要多點時間上網找資料。

❸ I'm glad I helped. → 很高興我幫上忙。

❹ Why don't you give her a call and tell her the truth?

→ 你為何不打給她，跟她說實話呢？

❺ Thanks for the advice. It helps a lot.

→ 謝謝你的建議，非常有用。

常見錯誤不要犯

在鼓勵別人去主動搭話的時候，可能會覺得有「說」的意思就好了，下意識脫口而出 "Just go speak to her." 但這是錯誤的說法。

正確的說法是 "Just go talk to her."

speak 和 talk 都有「說話」的意思。但 speak 一般比較廣，而且後面跟語言，如 speak English, speak Chinese。而 talk 一般有具體的內容，有交談、聊天的意思。

常見句型一起學

★ 委婉否定句

I　　don't　think　it's gonna work.

主詞　＋　否定助動詞　＋　動詞　＋　　　　子句

這個句型的重點在於，要表達否定意味時，「don't」要放在主句，這樣的用法比較委婉， 也是美語人士慣用的說話方式；若是把「don't」放在子句上，則語氣會太過強烈，非常不建議這樣使用。

以下是其他的相關例句：

▶ **I don't think I'll get promoted.**
→ 我不覺得我會升遷。

▷ **I don't think your plan will work.**
→ 我不覺得你的計畫可行。

▶ **I don't think he'll be here on time.**
→ 我不覺得他會準時到達。

▷ **She doesn't think he is a good father.**
→ 她不覺得他是個好爸爸。

▶ **They don't think you are on the right track.**
→ 他們不覺得你們在正軌上。

07 你喜歡外食嗎

 情境對話　🎧 Track 07

和朋友聊天的時候，會與對方聊及平時的日常生活，討論彼此的生活習慣，這時候就可以發現出彼此的習慣差異，甚至是文化差異。但要是對方的生活習慣和你不同，也千萬不要出言嘲笑喔。

A: Do you like to eat out every day?	你喜歡外食嗎？
B: No, I don't. But I have to.	不喜歡啊，但是我必須餐餐在外面解決。
A: Why? Because you're not a good cook?	為什麼？是因為你不會做菜嗎？
B: You've got it. I can't even tell salt from sugar.	答對了！我連鹽和糖都分不清楚呢。
A: Haha! It's hilarious.	哈哈！你很好笑耶！
B: What's so funny about that? I'm serious.	有什麼好笑的？我是很嚴肅地在說這件事耶。
A: Maybe you can learn how to cook. It can be fun.	或許你可以學著做飯啊，它可以很有趣的。
B: Perhaps you are right. I'll try some other day.	或許你是對的。改天我試試。

 關鍵單字要認得

eat out
ph. 外食

I don't need to eat out because my dad makes dinner everyday.
→ 我不用吃外食，因為我爸爸會每天煮晚餐。

cook	**Sarah wants to be a cook in the future.**
n. 廚師	→ 莎拉未來想成為廚師。
tell ... from	**I can't tell John from David. They are twins.**
ph. 分辨	→ 我沒辦法分辨約翰和大衛。他們是雙胞胎。
serious	**I'm serious about going to study abroad.**
adj. 嚴肅的；認真的	→ 我對出國留學這件事是認真的。

 一定要會的萬用句

① You've got it! → 答對了！

② It's hilarious. → 你很好笑耶！

③ What's so funny about that?

→ 有什麼好笑的？

④ It can be fun.

→ 它可以很有趣的。

 我們也能這樣說

① Do you like to eat in every day?

→ 你喜歡每天在家吃飯嗎？

② I love eating in. My mom is the best cook in the whole world.

→ 我喜歡在家吃飯。我媽是全世界最棒的廚師。

③ Because I'm not good at cooking, I have to eat out a lot.

→ 因為我不太會做菜，所以要常常在外面吃。

④ Bingo! → 答對了！

⑤ She can't tell which is which.

→ 她分不出哪個是哪個。

常見錯誤不要犯

當提到從事某些職業的人時，通常只要在後面加er就行了，但這個法則在cook上卻是錯誤的，因此 "Because you're not a good cooker?" 是錯誤的句子。

正確的説法是 "Because you're not a good cook?"

cook 和 cooker 是經常被弄混的兩個單字。首先一定要區分開兩者的意思：cook 是「廚師、炊事員」；而 cooker 是指「炊具、爐灶」。

常見句型一起學

★ 日常句型

What is so funny about that?

疑問詞 + be 動詞 + so + 形容詞 + 介系詞 + 受詞

這是一個很口語化的日常句型，依照語氣與上下文，有時會帶點不以為然的意味。

以下是其他的相關例句：

▶ **What is so special about that?**
→ 那有什麼特別的嗎？

▶ **What is so good about that?**
→ 那有什麼好的嗎？

▶ **What is so wonderful about that?**
→ 那有那麼棒嗎？

▶ **What is so hard about that?**
→ 那有什麼難的嗎？

▶ **What is so bad about that?**
→ 那有什麼不好的嗎？

08 抱歉，我一定是聽錯了

 情境對話　∩ **Track 08**

若因為聽錯別人的話，因此產生誤會，這種時候就要好好跟對方道歉，釐清對方的意思。

A: Are you taking the day off?	你休假嗎？
B: No. Now I'm unemployed.	不，我失業了。
A: I didn't know you were fired. What happened?	我不知道你被革職了。發生什麼事了？
B: They didn't fire me. I quit.	我沒有被革職。是我自己辭職的。
A: Oh, I'm so sorry. I must have heard it wrong. But why did you quit your job?	噢，真抱歉。我一定是聽錯了。不過你為什麼要辭職？
B: Because I did not want to be stuck in a dead-end job.	因為我不想待在一個沒有發展性的工作上。
A: I see. But what are you going to do now?	我瞭解。不過你現在有何打算？
B: Don't worry. I've landed a job at StarTrek Co.	別擔心。我在星際公司找到一份工作了。

 關鍵單字要認得

unemployed *adj.* 失業的	**Luke has been unemployed for two years.** → 路克已經失業兩年了。

fire

☑ 開除、革職

Sarah was fired last month.
→ 莎拉上個月被開除了。

quit

☑ 辭職

Amy quit her job to take care of her mom.
→ 艾咪辭掉工作以照顧她的媽媽。

dead-end

adj 無發展性的

This is a dead-end job. You should turn down the offer.
→ 這是沒有發展性的工作。你應該拒絕這份工作。

worry

☑ 擔心

Parents are always worried about their kids.
→ 父母總是擔心他們的小孩。

land

☑ 弄到、獲得

He landed a job last year.
→ 他去年找到工作了。

- -

 一定要會的萬用句

❶ Are you taking the day off? → 你休假嗎？

❷ I quit. → 我辭職了。

❸ I must have heard it wrong. → 我一定是聽錯了。

❹ I did not want to be stuck in a dead-end job.
→ 我不想待在一個沒有發展性的工作上。

 我們也能這樣說

❶ I didn't know you're married. → 我不知道你已婚。

❷ I'm not Mrs. Chen. I'm Miss Chen. I'm single.
→ 我不是陳太太，我是陳小姐。我還沒結婚。

❸ You must have said something wrong. → 你一定是説錯話了。

❹ She put her foot in her mouth. → 她失言了。

❺ Never mind. → 沒關係。

常見錯誤不要犯

當想要詢問發生什麼事時，並不是只要有happen在句中就好，還要注意那是不是一個完整的句子，因此"What happening?"是錯誤的。

正確的說法是"What happened?"

詢問「怎麼了？」、「發生什麼事了？」可以說：What happened? 或者 What's happening?。注意如果用 happen 的現在分詞形式的話，那麼一定要有 be 動詞。

常見句型一起學

★ 日常句型

I must have heard it wrong.

主詞 + must + have + p.p + 受詞 + 受詞補語

這個句型裡有完成式，所以是指已經發生過的事，表示「一定是……了」，強調做過的事，依照上下文及語氣，有時會帶有遺憾的意味。

以下是其他的相關例句：

▶ **I must have said something wrong.**
→ 我一定是說錯話了。

▶ **He must have loved you.**
→ 他一定愛過你。

▶ **She must have fallen asleep.**
→ 她一定是睡著了。

▶ **It must have rained.**
→ 一定下過雨。

▶ **They must have been here.**
→ 他們一定來過這裡。

 情境對話 ∩ Track 09

發現好友面露喜色，就可以問問他發生了什麼好事，與對方一起慶祝。像這樣共同分享生活大小事，就是增進感情的好方法！

A: Why are you so happy today?	你今天怎麼那麼高興啊？
B: I passed my calculus exam!	我通過微積分的考試了！
A: Wow, good for you! Now you can relax and get some sleep.	哇，好樣的！現在你可以放輕鬆睡一下了。
B: Yeah. I never thought I could pass the exam. I was so nervous!	對啊。我沒想到可以及格。我好緊張呢！
A: I always know you could do it. You worked really hard on it.	我一直都知道你會及格，因為你真的很用功。
B: Thanks! Ah, I totally need some sleep now!	謝了！啊，我現在真的得好好睡一覺了！
A: You sure do. Go get some rest now. You look pale!	沒錯。快去休息吧。你臉色好蒼白呢！

 關鍵單字要認得

pass ☑ 通過	**I hope I can pass the test.** → 我希望可以通過考試。

calculus
n. 微積分

John isn't good at calculus.
→ 約翰不擅長微積分。

exam
n. 考試

Sarah needs to prepare for the exam next month.
→ 莎拉要準備下個月的考試。

relax
v. 放鬆

I need a vacation to relax.
→ 我需要一個假期來放鬆。

nervous
adj. 緊張的

Sarah is nervous about the exam next month.
→ 莎拉為下個月的考試感到緊張。

rest
n. 休息

He needs to have a rest for a while.
→ 他需要休息一段時間。

- -

 一定要會的萬用句

① Why are you so happy today?
→ 你今天怎麼那麼高興啊？

❷ I passed my exam! → 我通過考試了！

❸ You worked really hard on it. → 你真的很用功。

❹ I totally need some sleep now!
→ 我現在真的得好好睡一覺了！

 我們也能這樣說

① I passed the audition! → 我通過試鏡了！

❷ Way to go! → 做得好啊！

❸ You deserve it. → 這是你應得的。

❹ It is too good to be true. → 簡直像在作夢一般。

❺ Well done. → 做得很好。

看到人臉色蒼白的時候，可能會下意識脫口而出 "You look white!"，但這是錯誤的。

正確的說法是 "You look pale!"

雖然 white 和 pale 都有「白的」的 意思。但是 white 一般指「白色的、白種的、純潔的」的意思；而 pale 指的是「蒼白的、灰白的、暗淡的、無力的」。形容人「面色蒼白」應該用 pale 而不能用 white。

常見句型一起學

★ 認為的事情與現在情形相反

I　　never　　thought　　I could pass the exam.

主詞　+　never　+　動詞過去式　+　　子句（助動詞過去式）

這個句型是用來表示「認為的事情與現在情形相反」的狀況，所以使用過去式，因為現在 知道真正的情形，所以是指「過去」認為的事。

以下是其他的相關例句：

▶ **I never thought I could land a good job.**
→ 我以為我絕對不會得到好工作。

▶ **He never thought he could make it.**
→ 他以為自己絕不會達成任務。

▶ **She never thought she would love him so much.**
→ 她以為自己絕不會愛他那麼深。

▶ **They never thought they would win.**
→ 他們以為自己絕對不會獲勝。

▶ **We never thought we could get there.**
→ 我們以為自己絕對走不到那裡。

10 通話的收訊很差

線上視訊或通話受限於網路訊號，若是訊號不好的話，無論是視訊或通話都很困難，這個時候或許就要換一個方式傳達彼此的意思，像是轉而傳訊息就會是比較不容易出錯的方式。

A: Sorry. Can you repeat that? The connection's bad.	抱歉，你可以再說一次嗎？收訊很差。
B: I said we can play the online game together after work.	我說我們工作結束後可以一起玩線上遊戲。
A: But I won't get off work until nine.	可是我要到九點才能下班耶。
B: Hello? Are you still there? I can't hear a thing!	喂？你還在嗎？我完全聽不到聲音！
A: I can't hear you clearly, either. I'll call you back in a few minutes.	我也聽得不是很清楚。我過幾分鐘再打給你好了。
B: Or you can send me a message.	或者你也可以傳訊息給我。
A: Alright.	好吧。

關鍵單字要認得

repeat ☑ 重複	**Please repeat after me.** → 請跟著我一起念。

connection
n. 收訊

The connection is very bad, so I'll call you later.
→ 收訊很糟，我晚點再打給你。

call sb. back
ph. 回某人電話

I'll call you back later.
→ 我等等會再打電話給你。

message
n. 訊息；消息

Do you get my message?
→ 你有收到我的訊息嗎？

 一定要會的萬用句

❶ Can you repeat that? → 你可以再說一次嗎？

❷ The connection's bad. → 收訊很差。

❸ I can't hear a thing! → 我完全聽不到聲音！

❹ I'll call you back in a few minutes.
→ 我過幾分鐘再打給你好了。

 我們也能這樣說

❶ Could you say that again?
→ 麻煩你再說一次好嗎？

❷ I can hardly hear you.
→ 我幾乎聽不到你的聲音。

❸ There's too much static.
→ 雜訊太多了。

❹ There's something wrong with my cellphone.
→ 我的手機有問題。

❺ I'll call again later.
→ 我等一下再打一次。

常見錯誤不要犯

在提到下班的時候，千萬不要覺得out of work看上去是離開工作，就認為這是下班，而說出 "But I won't be out of work until nine." 的錯誤句子。

正確的說法是 "But I won't get off work until nine."

out of work的意思其實是指「失業」，get off work才是「下班」的意思，或者口語一點說是be off也是可以的。

常見句型一起學

★ 要直到……才會……

I   won't get off work   until   nine.

主詞 ＋ won't ＋   動詞   ＋ until ＋ 時間點

這是個常用的句型，表示「要直到……才會……」的意思。

以下是其他的相關例句：

▶ **They won't leave until they get their money.**
→ 他們拿不到錢不會走。

▷ **He won't eat until dinnertime.**
→ 他不到晚餐時間不吃東西。

▶ **She won't pay the bill until next week.**
→ 她要到下週才會付帳單。

▷ **I won't sleep until midnight.**
→ 不到午夜我不會睡。

▶ **The show won't begin until five.**
→ 五點節目才會開始。

11 你終於上線了

當與家人身處異地，甚至是在不同國度的時候，透過網路聯絡就是最快最即時的辦法了。藉由網路，可以與身在異國的家人見面，交換彼此的近況，關心對方的生活，也可以問問對方什麼時候想要回家。

A: Hi! You're online at last! I haven't heard from you for a month!	嗨！你終於上線了！我已經一個月沒有你的消息了！
B: Hi, Sis! How's it going? I've been busy sightseeing in Paris.	嗨，老姊！最近好嗎？我一直忙著在巴黎觀光啊。
A: I thought you would be homesick.	我還以為你會很想家呢。
B: Yeah, I was homesick at first. But now I'm getting used to my life in Paris.	對啊，一開始我的確很想家，但是我現在已經逐漸適應在巴黎的生活了。
A: Speaking of Paris, how is your French going? Has it improved a lot?	說到巴黎，你的法文學得如何了？有沒有進步很多？
B: It sure has. You know, practice makes perfect!	當然有啦！你知道的，勤能補拙嘛！
A: Oh, I am happy for you. By the way, when will you come home?	噢，我真為你高興。對了，你什麼時候回家啊？
B: Maybe on Christmas.	可能聖誕節吧。

 關鍵單字要認得

at last
ph. 終於、總算

I passed the test at last.
→ 我終於通過考試了。

sightsee v. 觀光	**John want to sightsee in Paris.** → 約翰想在巴黎觀光。
homesick adj. 想家的	**Harry felt homesick when he studied abroad.** → 當哈利在國外念書時，他很想家。
getting used to ph. 習慣於	**Sarah is getting used to her life in England.** → 莎拉習慣她在英國的生活。
speaking of ph. 提到、説到	**Speaking of lunch, what did you have for lunch?** → 説到午餐，你午餐吃了什麼？
improve v. 改善、增進	**The best way to improve French was to live in France.** → 讓法文進步的最好方式是住在法國。

 一定要會的萬用句

❶ You're online at last! → 你終於上線了！

❷ I haven't heard from you for a month!

　　→ 我已經一個月沒有你的消息了！

❸ How's It going? → 最近好嗎？

❹ I'm getting used to my life in Paris.

　　→ 我已經逐漸適應在巴黎的生活了。

 我們也能這樣說

❶ Do you speak German? → 你會説德文嗎？

❷ My Italian isn't very good. → 我的義大利文不是很好。

❸ I don't speak Spanish. → 我不會説西班牙文。

❹ Do you know Chinese? → 你懂中文嗎？

❺ I speak a little English. → 我會説一點英文。

常見錯誤不要犯

在英文中，要注意是否需要使用介係詞，因此 "I haven't heard you for a month!"是錯誤的。

正確的說法是 "I haven't heard from you for a month!"

片語 hear from 意為「得到消息、收到……的信」。單字 hear 僅僅是「聽到」的意思。二者表達的意思完全不同。

常見句型一起學

★ ……怎麼樣了？

How is your French going?

How + be 動詞 + 主詞 + going

「How is ... going?」是口語中一個超級好用的句型，它可以套入各種名詞，例如你正在學習的東西或進行的事物、一個日子或季節，或者直接帶入「it」。

以下是其他的相關例句：

▶ **How is your job hunting going?**
→ 你的工作找得如何？

▶ **How is your summer going?**
→ 你的夏天過得如何？

▶ **How is your weekend going?**
→ 你的週末過得如何？

▶ **How is it going?**
→ 你好嗎？

▶ **How is your work going?**
→ 你的工作進行得如何？

12 你有算命的習慣嗎

藉由網路，可以更容易與不同國家的人接觸，在與不同國家的人交流的時候，很可能會聊到彼此的文化差異，要小心別批評不同的風俗習慣，才能讓談話更開心喔。

A: People in our country have the habit of visiting fortune tellers.	我們國家的人有給別人算命的習慣。
B: I didn't know that. Are you serious?	我都不知道耶，你是說真的嗎？
A: Yeah. And It has become a custom. I'd visited one myself and asked her about my career.	對啊。而且這已經變成一種習俗了。我自己也去算過命，問了算命師有關我的工作。
B: Did any of her predictions come true?	那個算命師的預測準嗎？
A: Not really. But you never know. Sometimes it's good to get some advice on your future.	不大準。不過世事難料。有時聽取一些對未來的建議也不錯。
B: I prefer not to think about the future but enjoy the present!	我寧可不去想未來，而是活在當下。

 關鍵單字要認得

have the habit of *ph.* 有⋯⋯的習慣	**I have the habit of taking a shower in the morning.** → 我有在早上洗澡的習慣。

fortune teller *n.* 算命師	**The fortune teller said that he would become a teacher.** → 算命師說他會成為老師。
custom *n.* 習俗、風俗	**Celebrating Christmas is a custom in Western society.** → 慶祝聖誕節是西方社會的習俗。
career *n.* 事業	**I'm worried about his career in America.** → 我擔心他在美國的事業。
prediction *n.* 預測	**The prediction of fortune teller didn't come true last time.** → 算命師上次說的預言沒有成真。
come true *ph.* 成真	**I hope my dream will come true one day.** → 希望我的願望總有一天會成真。

• •

 一定要會的萬用句

❶ Are you serious? → 你是說真的嗎？

❷ It has become a custom.

　　→ 這已經變成一種習俗了。

❸ Did any of her predictions come true?

　　→ 那個算命師的預測準嗎？

 我們也能這樣說

❶ I want to know about my future. → 我想知道我的未來。

❷ Tell me about my love life. → 告訴我有關我的感情生活。

❸ Will I be married? → 我會結婚嗎？

❹ How many kids will I have? → 我會有幾個小孩？

❺ Will I be rich? → 我會成為有錢人嗎？

常見錯誤不要犯

在討論夢想的時候，也要注意文法的問題，"Did any of her predictions came true?" 就犯了文法錯誤。

正確的說法是 "Did any of her predictions come true?"

片語 come true 意為「實現、成真」。此句中容易犯的錯誤是個文法錯誤。當前面已有表明過去時態的助動詞 did 的時候，後面的動詞無需再用過去式，而用動詞原形。

👍 **常見句型一起學**

★ 寧可不⋯⋯

I   prefer not to think about   the future.

主詞 + prefer + not +   不定詞   +   受詞 +（其他補語）

這是個包含「prefer」的句型，留意否定時「not」放置的位子，這是考試出題率高的句型。

以下是其他的相關例句：

▶ **She prefers not to mention her past.**
→ 她寧可不去提她的過去。

▶ **He prefers not to talk about it.**
→ 他寧可不去談論這件事。

▶ **They prefer not to sing the song.**
→ 他們寧可不去唱這首歌。

▶ **We prefer not to join them.**
→ 我們寧可不去加入他們。

▶ **I prefer not to worry about him.**
→ 我寧可不去擔心他。

13 這一定是謠言

謠言因為真假難辨，求證的難度高，使謠言難以被遏止，萬一是和身邊朋友有關的謠言，很可能會對他人造成傷害，因此對事實求證是相當重要的，一起成為停止散播謠言的智者吧！

A: I just learned some big news! Are you interested?	我剛聽到個大消息！你有興趣嗎？
B: What is it?	什麼消息啊？
A: I heard Joey is dating your ex-girlfriend, Sharon.	我聽說喬伊跟你的前女友雪倫正在交往。
B: Who did you hear it from?	你從誰那裡聽來的？
A: I can't tell you. But definitely not from Joey. He doesn't know that we know.	我不能告訴你，但肯定不是從喬伊那裡聽來的。他還不知道我們知道他們的事情。
B: Do you have proof? I bet that's just a rumor.	你有證據嗎？這一定只是謠言。
A: Is it? But I don't think so.	是嗎？但我不這麼認為。
B: Get your nose out of other people's business, OK? Don't you have better things to do?	你少管別人家的閒事，好嗎？你沒有別的事情好做了嗎？

 關鍵單字要認得

date
☑ 與……約會

Mary is dating my brother.
→ 瑪麗在和我弟弟約會。

ex-girlfriend
n. 前女友

John doesn't want to see his ex-girlfriend again.
→ 約翰不想再見到他前女友。

definitely
adv. 肯定地

I can't definitely sure what he wants.
→ 我不確定他想要什麼。

proof
n. 證據

Amy didn't have any proof that David cheated on the test.
→ 艾咪沒有任何證據證明大衛考試作弊。

rumor
n. 謠言

I heard a rumor that the president left for America.
→ 我聽到一個謠言說總統去美國了。

nose
n. 鼻子

He broke his nose during the basketball game.
→ 在籃球比賽的時候他鼻子骨折了。

• •

 一定要會的萬用句

❶ I just learned some big news! → 我剛聽到個大消息！

❷ Are you interested? → 你有興趣嗎？

❸ Who did you hear it from? → 你從誰那裡聽來的？

❹ Get your nose out of other people's business!
→ 少管別人家的閒事！

 我們也能這樣說

❶ Did you hear about Cindy and her boyfriend?
→ 你有聽說辛蒂和她男友的事情嗎？

❷ We are through. → 我們之間結束了。

❸ I knew it would come to this. → 我就知道結局會是如此。

❹ They are meant for each other. → 他們是天生佳偶。

❺ He's been cheating on her. → 他一直都背著她跟別人交往。

常見錯誤不要犯

在有重大新聞想要分享的時候,也要注意文法的問題,"I have a big news." 就犯了文法錯誤。

正確的說法是 "I have some big news."

news 意為「新聞、消息」,字尾的 s 會讓人誤以為是複數,但實際上卻是單數。所以前面不能加不定冠詞 a。注意 some 不僅有「一些」的意思,還有「某個」的意思。

常見句型一起學

★ 介係詞相關句型

Who   did   you   hear   it   from?

疑問詞 + 助動詞 + 主詞 + 動詞 + 受詞 + 介系詞

這是非常重要的句型,很多國人受到中文思維的影響,使用疑問句型時,通常會忘了加上該有的介系詞。

以下是其他的相關例句:

▶ **Where do you come from?**
→ 你來自哪裡?

▶ **What do you want it for?**
→ 你要這個做什麼?

▶ **Who do you borrow it from?**
→ 你跟誰借的?

▶ **Who did you lend it to?**
→ 你借給誰?

▶ **Who do you work for?**
→ 你為誰工作?

14 好久不見

 情境對話 ∩ **Track 14**

與好久不見的朋友重逢時，可以交換彼此的近況，了解對方生活中有沒有什麼重大的改變，也能趁這個時候再加深彼此的感情。

A: Hi, Kevin!	嗨，凱文！
B: Hi, Alice! Long time no see!	嗨，愛麗絲！好久不見！
A: I know! What's new?	是啊！你近況如何呢？
B: Well, I just got married.	嗯，我剛結婚。
A: Congratulations!	恭喜你！
B: Thank you. What about you?	謝謝妳，那妳呢？
A: Still single. I guess you could say I'm married to my job!	還是單身。我想你可以說我嫁給了工作。

 關鍵單字要認得

Long time no see! *ph.* 好久不見	**Long time no see! How's it going?** → 好久不見，你過得怎麼樣？
Congratulations *n.* 恭喜、祝賀	**You got a job! Congratulations!** → 你找到工作了！恭喜！
single *adj.* 單身的、未婚的	**John is single now.** → 約翰現在單身。

| **guess**
☑ 猜測 | **I guess Amy forgot the test.**
→ 我猜艾咪忘記要考試了。 |
| **marry**
☑ 結婚 | **He got married last year.**
→ 他去年結婚了。 |

- -

 一定要會的萬用句

❶ Long time no see! → 好久不見！

❷ What's new? → 你近況如何呢？

❸ I just got married. → 我剛結婚。

❹ Still single. → 還是單身。

 我們也能這樣說

❶ It's been a long time. → 好久不見了。

❷ How long has it been since I last met you?

　　→ 從上次見面到現在，已經有多久了？

❸ It has been at least five years!

　　→ 至少有五年了！

❹ Where does the time go?

　　→ 時間過得真快，是吧？

❺ I'm married with three kids.

　　→ 我結婚了，而且有三個小孩了。

❻ No lucky guy? → 沒有適合的對象嗎？

❼ No one special in your life?

　　→ 生命中沒遇到特別的對象嗎？

常見錯誤不要犯

英語也有像中文的成語一般的慣用語，使用的時候要注意，如 "Long time no saw." 就是錯誤的。

正確的說法是 "Long time no see."

Long time no see. 意思是「好久不見、好長時間沒有看到你了」
LTNS 為其縮寫形式。Long time no see. 是固定的表達方式，
不能用 Long time no saw。

常見句型一起學

★「get＋過去分詞」的口語表達

I　got　married.

主詞 ＋ get ＋ 過去分詞

「get＋過去分詞」是一種口語表達，可以用來代替「be 動詞＋過去分詞」。但是，兩者之間仍然有些許的差異，「get＋過去分詞」較常用來表示突發性的事件，且帶有較強烈的感情色彩，例如：

▶ **I got hurt on my way to school.**
→ 我在上學途中受傷了。

「get＋過去分詞」看起來雖然是一種被動形式，但其實也可以用來表示主動的意義，例如：get married（結婚）、get lost（迷路）等，都是主動形式。至於被動形式的例子，則有：get confused（被搞糊塗了）、get broken（被打破了）等。

15 你過得怎麼樣

情境對話 🎧 Track 15

好朋友不一定會天天和對方聊天說話,但是總會定期關心對方,在有便捷的網路之後,關心朋友也更容易了。可以透過網路,定期與朋友聯絡,關心對方的狀況。

A: Hi! How have you been?	嗨!你近來過得怎麼樣?
B: Couldn't be better. I haven't seen you for a while. Is everything alright?	好到不能再好。我有一段時間沒看到你了,一切還好嗎?
A: I just have so much on my plate right now.	現在我有好多事要忙。
B: Such as?	忙什麼呢?
A: I'm really busy at work. I feel like I'm doing the job of three people! I've been really run-down lately.	我的工作實在很忙,我覺得自己好像在做三人份的工作,我最近一直覺得精疲力盡。
B: You really have to take good care of yourself. Don't get sick.	你真的應該好好照顧自己,別生病了。
A: Thanks for your concern. I know I can always count on you!	謝謝你的關心,我知道你永遠是可以信賴的朋友。

 關鍵單字要認得

plate 🔢 盤子	**She was angry at her son because he broke the plate.** → 她因為兒子打破盤子而對他生氣。

take good care of _ph._ 好好照顧	**John took good care of himself in Paris.** → 約翰在巴黎的時候把自己照顧得很好。
get sick _ph._ 生病	**Harry hates to get sick.** → 哈利痛恨生病。
concern _n._ 關懷	**Thanks for your concern. I'm glad we are friends.** → 謝謝你的關心。我很高興我們是朋友。
count on _ph._ 信賴	**He is your best friend, so you can count on him.** → 他是你最好的朋友，所以你可以信賴他。

• •

 一定要會的萬用句

❶ How have you been? → 你近來過得怎麼樣？

❷ Couldn't be better. → 好到不能再好。

❸ I just have so much on my plate right now. → 我現在有好多事要忙。

❹ I know I can always count on you! → 我知道你永遠是可以信賴的朋友。

 我們也能這樣說

❶ I haven't spoken to you for a while. → 我有一段時間沒和你聊聊了。

❷ There's just so much going on in my life right now.

　　→ 我現在每天都忙著做好多事。

❸ I'm too tired to even pick up the cellphone to chat.

　　→ 我甚至累到無法拿起手機和朋友聊聊天。

❹ I'm always here if you need a friend.

　　→ 當你需要朋友時，我都會在你身邊。

❺ I can always rely on you. → 我可以永遠信賴你。

❻ I can always depend on you. → 我可以永遠信賴你。

you和yourself之間的差異可能會害人混淆，而說出 "You really have to take good care of you." 的錯誤句子。

正確的說法是 "You really have to take good care of yourself."

片語 take good care of 意為「好好照顧」。此句要表達「好好照顧你自己」，所以 of 後面的受詞需為 yourself 而不是 you。

 常見句型一起學

★ 現在完成式：「have＋過去分詞」

I　have　been　really run-down lately.

主詞　＋　have　＋　過去分詞　＋　　其他補充語

「have＋過去分詞」的句型是屬於現在完成式，表示「過去」發生的事，直到「現在」才完成，有「從過去某個時間點到現在，一直都是如此」的意涵，例如：

▶ **I have lived here for ten years.**

→ 我住在這裡已經十年了。

如果是否定形式的話，就必須在「have」後面加「not」，例如：

▶ **I have not seen you for a while.**

→ 我有一段時間沒看到你了。

▶ **I have not seen him for ages.**

→ 我很久沒見到他了。

16 我還是老樣子

網路可以幫助我們重新聯繫許久不見的老朋友,但若老朋友不常在社群網站上更新自己的近況,那很可能就會不清楚對方生命中的重大改變。在聊天時,除了關心對方的生活,也要小心不要冒犯到對方喔。

A: Hey. How are you?	嗨。你好嗎?
B: Not bad. And you?	還不錯,你呢?
A: It's the same ol' same ol'.	還是老樣子啦。
B: So, you're still working in the same company and still dating with the same girl?	所以,你還是在同一家公司上班,和同一個女孩約會囉?
A: Actually, I broke up with her last year.	其實,我去年跟她分手了。
B: Oh, I'm sorry to hear that. But why?	哦,聽到這個消息我很遺憾。但是為什麼呢?
A: Because we both think we are not the right person to each other.	因為我們倆都認為彼此不是對的那個人。

 關鍵單字要認得

same *adj.* 同樣的	**This is the same book as I bought yesterday.** → 這本書和我昨天買的書是同一本。

same ol' same ol' *ph.* 老樣子	**Nothing changes. Everything here is the same ol' same ol'.** → 什麼都沒有改變。這個地方還是老樣子。
date with *ph.* 與……交往	**Harry is dating his classmate.** → 哈利在跟他的同學交往。
actually *adv.* 事實上	**Actually, John still stays in the city.** → 事實上，約翰還住在城市裡。
break up with *ph.* 與……分手	**Mary doesn't want to break up with her boyfriend.** → 瑪麗不想和她的男朋友分手。

• •

 一定要會的萬用句

❶ Not bad. → 還不錯。

❷ It's the same ol' same ol'. → 還是老樣子啦。

❸ I broke up with her last year. → 我去年跟她分手了。

❹ I'm sorry to hear that. → 聽到這個消息我很遺憾。

 我們也能這樣說

❶ How is it going? → 你好嗎？

❷ How's everything going? → 事情進行得順利嗎？

❸ How's life treating you? → 日子過得好嗎？

❹ What's up with you? → 你最近好嗎？

❺ The same as usual. → 跟往常一樣囉。

❻ Some things never change. → 有些事是不會變的啦！

😲 常見錯誤不要犯

在英文中，介係詞是一個句子中很重要的存在，若是忽略介係詞就可能說出
"I broke up her last year." 的錯誤句子。

正確的說法是 "I broke up with her last year."

片語 break up 意為「分手」；片語 break up with... 意為「與……分手」。
如果表達的意思是「和……分手」，那麼一定要有介係詞 with。

👍 常見句型一起學

★「be 動詞 + 現在分詞」構成進行式

You   are   working   in the same company.

主詞 ＋ be 動詞 ＋ 現在分詞 ＋ 其他補充語

「be 動詞 + 現在分詞」所構成的句子是進行式，表示「某事或某物正在……」，
現在進行式用來表示現在正在進行的動作，後面常接 now、still、at this time。

以下是其他的相關例句：

▶ **I am working in the same company.**
→ 我在同一家公司上班。

▶ **He is working in a big company.**
→ 他在一家大公司上班。

▶ **I am waiting for you at the coffee shop.**
→ 我正在那家咖啡店等你。

17 你需要幫忙嗎

在生活中，難免會碰到需要其他人幫助的事，若是住在同一個城市，見面容易的話可以趕去幫忙，但若是相隔遙遠，也就只能關心對方的狀況和進度，想想看自己有沒有什麼資源可以提供。

A: I'll be moving into my new apartment next week.	我下星期要搬進我的新公寓。
B: Do you need any help?	你需要幫忙嗎？
A: No, my brother hired movers and they gave him a good price.	不用，我哥哥有雇用搬家工人，而且他們收費很合理。
B: Speaking of your brother, what's up with him?	說到你哥，他最近好嗎？
A: He's going to study abroad.	他要出國念書了。
B: That is his dream! He must be very excited.	那是他的夢想耶！他一定非常興奮。
A: Absolutely. I am also happy for him.	當然。我也為他高興。

 關鍵單字要認得

move into
ph. 搬進

I moved into the new apartment yesterday .
→ 我昨天搬進新公寓了。

hire
v. 雇用

The company should hire more employees .
→ 公司應該雇用更多員工。

mover n. 搬家工人	**Harry became a mover.** → 哈利成為一名搬家工人。
price n. 價格	**The price he asked is very low.** → 他開的價錢非常低。
abroad adv. 到國外	**Mary hopes to study abroad in the future.** → 瑪麗希望以後可以出國留學。

⭐ **一定要會的萬用句**

① Do you need any help? → 你需要幫忙嗎？

❷ Speaking of your brother, what's up with him?
→ 說到你哥，他最近好嗎？

③ He's going to study abroad. → 他要出國念書了。

 我們也能這樣說

① I'll hire movers to help me.
→ 我會雇用搬家工人來幫我。

❷ They gave me a good deal.
→ 他們給我不錯的價格。

③ Speaking of my sister, did you know she's pregnant?
→ 說到我姊，你知道她懷孕了嗎？

❹ He's really thrilled. → 他很興奮。

⑤ She's really delighted.
→ 她好高興。

❻ She's down. → 她情緒低落。

句子中會不會出現介係詞是學英文的一個重點，若是搞錯了就可能說出 "He's going to study in abroad." 的錯誤句子。

正確的說法是 "He's going to study abroad."

abroad 本身就有副詞詞性，意為「在國外、到海外」。所以直接說 study abroad 就好，中間無須再使用介係詞 in。

 常見句型一起學

★ 主詞為第一人稱／第二人稱／複數的疑問句型

Do   you   need any help?

助動詞 ＋ 主詞 ＋ 原形動詞

Do 放在句首，且句尾用問號，表示這是一個疑問句型，要注意的是，在主詞後面一定要接原形動詞。根據時態的不同，Do 也可能換成 Did（過去式）。例如：

▶ **Did you call your dad last night?**
→ 你昨晚有打電話給你爸嗎？

主詞是第三人稱單數（he / she / it / my friend / my dog...）時，Do 必須換成 Does，例如：

▶ **Does he speak Chinese?**
→ 他說中文嗎？

▶ **Does your husband treat you nice?**
→ 你老公對你好嗎？

18 天氣真好啊

 情境對話 🎧 Track 18

天氣與我們的生活息息相關，更是聊天的常見話題，不只是和朋友一起出遊的時候可以聊到，在網路上也可以！和網友聊天氣，是關心對方的生活，也是瞭解不同地方氣候的一種方式喔。

A: What a beautiful day! We certainly need more days like this.	天氣真好啊！我們的確需要多一點這種好天氣。
B: Yeah. Global warming has worried me. It seems that we never know how the weather will be.	是啊！全球暖化令我擔心，我們似乎無法預知氣候會如何。
A: And we can't always rely on weather reports now.	而且我們現在也不能總是依賴天氣預報。
B: Do your find your customers are happier on sunny days like today?	你有沒有發現你的客人在像今天這樣的好天氣時，比較開心？
A: Oh, yes. And they chat more.	哦，有啊！而且他們更會閒話家常呢。
B: Haha, that's because you are talkative!	哈哈，那是因為你很健談呀！

 關鍵單字要認得

certainly
adv. 確實

Parenting is certainly not easy.
→ 養育子女確實不簡單。

global
adj. 全球的

Protecting the environment from pollution is a global issue.
→ 保護環境不受汙染是全球議題。

rely on
ph. 依賴

You can rely on your friend.
→ 你可以依賴你的朋友。

weather report
ph. 天氣預報

You should check the weather report before the trip.
→ 在旅行前你應該先確認天氣預報。

chat
v. 聊天

They chat every night.
→ 他們每天晚上都會聊天。

- -

 一定要會的萬用句

① What a beautiful day! → 天氣真好啊！

② Global warming has worried me. → 全球暖化令我擔心。

③ We can't always rely on weather reports now.
→ 我們現在也不能總是依賴天氣預報。

④ You are talkative. → 你很健談。

 我們也能這樣說

① What a lovely day! → 天氣真好啊！

② How wonderful a day is! → 天氣真好啊！

③ Your parents worry about you. → 你的父母擔心你。

④ We never know what the weather will be like.
→ 我們不知道天氣將會是如何。

⑤ Who knows what will the weather be like?
→ 誰知道天氣將會是如何？

常見錯誤不要犯

感嘆句會使用How和What，但兩者不能通用，可能會因為混淆而出現 "How a beautiful day." 的錯誤句子。

正確的說法是"What a beautiful day!"

由 what 引出的感歎句其基本結構是「what + a (an) + 形容詞 + 名詞 + 主語 + 謂語」，如 What a clever boy he is! 他是多麼聰明的孩子呀。由 how 引出的感歎句基本結構是「how + 形容詞或副詞 + 主語 + 謂語」，如 How tall the man is! 那個人真高！

常見句型一起學

★ 似乎……

It   seems   that we never know how the weather will be.

主詞 +   seem   +   that 子句

seem 是動詞，指的是「似乎、看來好像要」，所以這個句型的含意是「某件事看起來似乎……」。

以下是其他的相關例句：

▶ **It seems that you've already got through it!**
→ 看來你似乎已經撐過去了！

▷ **It seems that we need to call the police.**
→ 我們似乎需要報警處理。

19 有什麼好事發生

當朋友分享生活中開心的事情，就可以跟對方一起慶祝，慰勞他的辛勞。聽對方說自己生活中的大小事，對促進感情非常有幫助喔。

A: Ben, you look so excited. What's the good news?	班，你看起來很興奮。有什麼好事啊？
B: I got it! I finally got the contract!	我辦到了！我終於拿到合約了！
A: Really?	真的嗎？
B: Yeah, finally!	是啊，終於！
A: Congrats! You have done so much for that.	恭喜你！你付出了好多心血。
B: You're right. I spent a lot of time dealing with the job.	你說對了，我花了好多時間在這個工作上。
A: You deserve it. I'm truly happy for you.	這是你應得的，我真為你感到高興。

 關鍵單字要認得

really *adv.* 真實地	**Do you really want to turn down the job offer?** → 你真的想要拒絕這份工作嗎？
finally *adv.* 終於	**I finally finish my homework.** → 我終於完成我的作業了。

| **deserve**
v. 應得 | **You deserve more than that.**
→ 你值得更好的。 |
| **truly**
adv. 真實地 | **The scenery here is truly beautiful.**
→ 這裡的景色是真的很美。 |

 一定要會的萬用句

❶ I got it! → 我辦到了！

❷ Congrats! → 恭喜你！

❸ You have done so much for that.

　　→ 你付出了好多心血。

❹ You deserve it.

　　→ 這是你應得的。

 我們也能這樣說

❶ You worked really hard for that.

　　→ 你真的付出了許多努力。

❷ It doesn't come easily, does it?

　　→ 這得來不易，不是嗎？

❸ I paid a high price for it.

　　→ 我付出了很高的代價。

❹ I can't agree more.

　　→ 我再同意不過了！（對極了！）

❺ I'm one happy camper!

　　→ 我好高興！

想要說這是一個人應得到某些報酬，或說某個人是有價值的，可能會順著「價值」聯想到worth，說出 "You worth it." 的錯誤句子。

正確的說法是 "You deserve it."

deserve 為動詞，意為「應受、應得、值得」；worth 有名詞「價值」，也有形容詞「值得的、值錢的」的意思。顯然這裡使用謂語動詞才能構成一個完整的句子。

常見句型一起學

★ 某人花時間做了某事

I   spent   a lot of time   dealing with the job.

主詞（人） + spend   +   時間   +   (V-ing) 動名詞

這個句型的意思是「某人花時間做了某事」，主詞必定是人，不可以是物，而且時間後面一定要接動名詞（V-ing）。例如：

▶ **He has spent years collecting stamps.**
→ 他花了好多年集郵。

如果要問別人「花了多久時間做某事」，則可以用 How many 或 How much 來問，例如：

▶ **How much time do you spend watching TV every day?**
　＝How many hours do you spend watching TV every day?
→ 你每天花幾小時看電視？

20 別跟我說話

 情境對話　∩ Track 20

當朋友分享生活中不開心的事情，就可以跟對方一起生氣，也能提供建議。聽對方說自己生活中的大小事，對促進感情非常有幫助喔。

A: Hi, Allan!	嗨，艾倫！
B: Don't talk to me!	別跟我說話！
A: Hey, what's wrong with you?	嘿，你怎麼啦？
B: I am so annoyed!	我好生氣！
A: What happened?	出什麼事了？
B: My girlfriend stood me up again!	我女朋友又放我鴿子了！
A: Too bad. Why not stand her up next time?	太糟了。何不下次換你放她鴿子？
B: Good idea. I never thought of that.	好主意，我從來都沒想過可以這麼做。

 關鍵單字要認得

wrong *adj.* 錯誤的、不對的	**The answer teacher told us is wrong.** → 老師告訴我們的答案是錯的。
annoyed *adj.* 惱怒的	**I was so annoyed with him for forgetting the date.** → 我很氣他忘記約會。

stand ... up	**I'm sorry for standing you up.**
ph. 放某人鴿子	→ 我很抱歉放你鴿子。

idea	**He always comes up with great ideas.**
n. 主意、點子	→ 他總是想到很棒的點子。

 一定要會的萬用句

❶ What's wrong with you?

→ 你怎麼啦？

❷ My girlfriend stood me up again!

→ 我女朋友又放我鴿子了！

❸ Too bad. → 太糟了。

❹ I never thought of that.

→ 我從來都沒想過可以這麼做。

 我們也能這樣說

❶ If you don't tell me the truth, I will be pissed off.

→ 如果你不告訴我實話，我會發飆的。

❷ He shouted in anger.

→ 他氣得大叫。

❸ I never thought of that.

→ 我從來都沒想過可以這麼做。

❹ It never came to my mind.

→ 我從來都沒想過。

❺ How come I never had this idea?

→ 我怎麼從來都沒這種想法？

常見錯誤不要犯

在英文中，受詞是相當重要的，決定了一個動作是對誰做的，因此 "My girlfriend stood up again!" 這樣沒有受詞的句子是錯誤的。

正確的說法是 "My girlfriend stood me up again!"

片語 stand up 意為「站起來、（論點、證據等）站得住腳」；片語 stand sb. up 意為「讓某人空等一場、放鴿子」。My girlfriend stood up again! 的中文意思是「我女朋友又站起來了！」

常見句型一起學

★ 為什麼不……？

Why not   stand   her up next time?

Why not　+　原形動詞　+　　　　其他

Why not...表示「何不、為什麼不……？」，雖然看起來好像是疑問句，但並不是真的希望對方回答，而是提出建議。

這是一個省略句型，not 其實是代替 don't you，所以原本的句子應該是 Why don't you stand her up next time? 也因此，not 的後面必定要接原形動詞。此外，not 也可以代替 don't we。

以下是其他的相關例句：

▶ **Why not tell him the truth?**
→ 何不告訴他實話？

▶ **Why not go shopping this evening?**
　＝Why don't we go shopping this evening?
→ 我們何不今晚去購物？

21 你看起來很傷心

當朋友分享生活中難過的事情時，可以安慰對方，為他排解憂煩，一起找一些開心的事情來做。

A: Are you alright? You look so sad. What happened?	你還好吧？你看起來很傷心。發生什麼事了嗎？
B: I just broke up with my boyfriend.	我剛和男朋友分手。
A: Oh, I can't believe it! How come?	噢，真不敢相信！怎麼會這樣？
B: I found he's dating another girl.	我發現他和另一個女孩約會。
A: He's such a jerk! He doesn't deserve your tears!	他真是個王八蛋！他不值得你為他掉淚。
B: You are right. Let's watch comedy movies together! I'm gonna forget him in a day.	你說得對，我們一起看喜劇電影吧！我要在一天之內忘記他！
A: OK. Let's go!	好的，走吧！

 關鍵單字要認得

believe ☑ 相信	**I believe that John will forgive you .** → 我相信約翰會原諒你的。
find ☑ 發現	**May found that Harry cheated at cards.** → 梅發現哈利玩牌時作弊。

jerk _n._ 王八蛋	**You're such a jerk!** → 你真是個王八蛋！
tear _n._ 眼淚	**She cries tears of joy.** → 她流下開心的淚水。

· ·

 一定要會的萬用句

❶ Are you alright? → 你還好吧？

❷ I just broke up with my boyfriend.

→ 我剛和男朋友分手。

❸ How come? → 怎麼會這樣？

❹ He's such a jerk! → 他真是個王八蛋！

 我們也能這樣說

❶ He blew up at his girl friend last night.

→ 他昨天和女朋友大吵一架。

❷ I am not going out with you again.

→ 我不會再跟你約會了。

❸ I can tell by your eyes you've been crying.

→ 從你的眼裡，我可以看得出來你哭過。

❹ I'm really sorry.

→ 我感到很遺憾。

❺ There are lots of guys out there who would love to date you.

→ 外面有許多男人想要和你約會。

在形容人或事物的時候，常常會搞混so和such的用法，說出 "He's so a jerk!" 這樣錯誤的句子。

正確的說法是 "He's such a jerk!"

so 的基本用法是：so + adj. / adv.，如：so beautiful「如此美麗的」；
such 的基本用法是：such + a (n) + n.，如：such a lovely girl.「多麼可愛的女孩」。

常見句型一起學

★ 讓我們⋯⋯

Let's   watch   comedy movies together!

Let's + 原形動詞 + 其他

Let's...是祈使句，表示「讓我們⋯⋯」，在提議或請求時，可以使用這個句型。要注意的是，Let's...後面一定要接原形動詞。此外，Let's...與 Let us...雖然看起來都是「讓我們⋯⋯」的意思，但兩者的含意還是不太相同。Let's 中的「我們」包括了說者自己和聽者，但 Let us 中的「我們」並不包括聽者在內。

以下是其他的相關例句：

▶ **Bill, let's go out for lunch!**
→ 比爾，我們去吃午餐吧！（在這個句子中，「我們」包含了比爾。）

▶ **Bill, let us go out for lunch!**
→ 比爾，讓我們其他人去吃午餐吧！（在這個句子中，「我們」不包含比爾。）

22 你最喜歡哪個明星

 情境對話 ∩ Track 22

在網路上認識新朋友的時候，可能會聊到彼此的興趣，而音樂可以說是非常好開啟話題的方式，可以聊聊彼此喜歡的音樂類型、歌手或樂團等，但在聊天的時候，要注意不要冒犯到對方的喜好喔。

A: Sara, who's your favorite star?	莎拉，妳最喜歡哪個明星啊？
B: I'm crazy about Jay Chou.	我好喜歡周杰倫。
A: Really? WHY?	真的嗎？為什麼？
B: He's very talented.	他很有才華。
A: I can't stand his voice. I don't think he can sing at all.	我受不了他的聲音，我認為他完全不會唱歌。
B: His voice is one of a kind.	他的聲音獨樹一格。
A: I don't think so.	我不這麼認為。

 關鍵單字要認得

crazy about *ph.* 為……瘋狂	**She is crazy about video games.** → 她為電動遊戲瘋狂。
talented *adj.* 有天分的	**David is a talented painter.** → 大衛是一個有天分的畫家。
stand *v.* 忍受	**I can't stand the noise anymore.** → 我不能再忍耐這噪音了。

voice

n. 聲音

Please raise your voice.
→ 請提高你的音量。

kind

n. 種類

What kind of fruit do you want?
→ 你想要什麼種類的水果？

 一定要會的萬用句

❶ I'm crazy about Jay Chou.

→ 我好喜歡周杰倫。

❷ He's very talented.

→ 他很有才華。

❸ I can't stand his voice.

→ 我受不了他的聲音。

❹ His voice is one of a kind.

→ 他的聲音獨樹一格。

 我們也能這樣說

❶ I made a love announcement to him.

→ 我向他告白了。

❷ What kind of style do you have?

→ 你具有什麼樣的風格？

❸ He has a talent for music.

→ 他具有音樂天賦。

❹ I'm totally crazy about keane.

→ 我為基音樂團瘋狂。

常見錯誤不要犯

在英文中，單字有詞性變化，如果沒有確定不同詞性的拼寫，
可能就會説出 "He's very talent." 這樣錯誤的句子。

正確的説法是 "He's very talented."

talent 是名詞，意為「才能、天資、人才」；talented 是形容詞，意為
「有才能的、有才華的」。用副詞 **very** 修飾的一定是形容詞，所以應
使用 talented。

👍 **常見句型一起學**

★ 否定後面的子句

I　　don't　think　he can sing at all.

主詞　+　否定　+　think　+　　　　子句

這是一個否定句，但否定的是後面的子句，也就是説，想表達的是「He can not
sing at all.」。但由於 think 是一種表示心理活動的動詞，所以習慣上會把否定詞 not
移到主句中，變成了 I don't think...，例如：

▶ **I don't think you can make it.**
→ 我不認為你會成功。

believe 跟 think 一樣，也是一種表示心理活動的動詞，所以否定詞也會移到主句
中，例如：

▶ **We don't believe that he can get a high score.**
→ 我們不相信他能得高分。

23 你還好嗎？

情境對話　🎧 **Track 23**

在朋友主動分享生活裡遇到的糟心事時，可以想辦法幫他換個角度來看事情，改用比較正面的角度來看的話，或許能夠一併趕跑糟糕的心情呢。

A: Why are you so depressed?	你怎麼這麼沮喪？
B: I was fired yesterday.	我昨天被炒魷魚了。
A: I'm sorry about that. Are you OK?	我很遺憾。你還好嗎？
B: Not at all. It's the first time I've ever been fired!	一點也不，這是我生平第一次被開除！
A: Don't beat yourself up about it. Look on the bright side. Now you can take that holiday you've been dreaming about for so long.	別被這件事擊垮了，往好處想，你現在可以好好享受你夢想已久的假期了。
B: That's true. I feel better now. Thanks for your concern.	這倒是真的。我覺得好多了，謝謝你的關心。
A: Don't mention it.	不客氣。

關鍵單字要認得

fire ☑ 開除	**He is afraid of being fired.** → 他害怕被開除。
not at all *ph.* 一點也不	**He's not happy at all about mistakes his son made.** → 他對自己兒子犯的錯很不開心。

beat yourself up *ph.* 責怪自己	**Don't beat yourself up. You can try again.** → 不要太責怪自己。你可以再試一次。
bright *adj.* 明亮的	**The room with windows is bright.** → 有窗戶的房間很亮。
mention *v.* 提及	**Did he mention that what should we do next?** → 他有提到我們接下來該做什麼嗎？

 一定要會的萬用句

1 Why are you so depressed? → 你怎麼這麼沮喪？

2 I was fired. → 我被炒魷魚了。

3 Not at all. → 一點也不。

4 Look on the bright side. → 往好處想。

 我們也能這樣說

1 Don't drive yourself crazy thinking about it.

→ 別一直想著這件事，而把自己逼瘋了。

2 I'm frustrated by my bad performance.

→ 我為自己差勁的表現感到挫敗。

3 It's not the end of the world. Cheer up!

→ 又不是世界末日，開心點！

4 You've done your best.

→ 你已經盡力了。

5 Think about your next move.

→ 想一想你的下一步要怎麼走。

常見錯誤不要犯

在英文中，被動用法中的動詞有沒有改成過去分詞是很重要的，
若是忽略這點就可能就會說出 "I was fire." 這樣錯誤的句子。

正確的說法是 "I was fired."

動詞變成過去分詞 (V-ed) 之後，便具有形容詞的特性。在此句中，
be 動詞後面不可再接動詞，必須將 fire 變成過去分詞 fired 才對。

常見句型一起學

★ 第……次做……

It   is   the first time I've ever been fired!

虛主詞 + be動詞 + the + 序數詞 + time +   that子句

這個句型的意思是「第……次做……」，其中的 that 子句通常使用現在完成式，而
且 that 可以省略，例如：

▶ **It is the first time that I have been here.**
  ＝**It is the first time I have been here.**
→ 這是我第一次到這裡來。

序數詞指的就是first（第一）、second（第二）、third（第三）……，例如：

▶ **This is the second time that I have seen you on the street.**
→ 這是我第二次在路上看到你。

▶ **This is the third time that I have seen you at school.**
→ 這是我第三次在學校看到你。

24 我決定開始學編織

培養了新的興趣後，就會想要跟志同道合的人一起分享，但身邊的人未必會感興趣。要與擁有共同興趣的人交流，從網路尋找相關社群是一個好方向。在網路上，即使是很冷門的興趣，也有機會找到同好。

A: I've decided to take up knitting.	我決定要開始學編織了。
B: Have you ever knitted anything before?	你以前編織過任何東西嗎？
A: No, never.	從來沒有。
B: Well, it's really "in" right now.	嗯，編織現在很流行。
A: Yeah and it looks easy enough.	對，而且它看起來很容易。
B: I guess it's no longer just your grandma's hobby!	我想這不再只是老奶奶的興趣了。
A: I can't agree with you more.	完全同意。

 關鍵單字要認得

knit ⓥ 編織	**She knitted a pair of gloves for me.** → 她織了一雙手套送我。
before *prep.* 之前	**He has breakfast before school.** → 他上學前先吃了早餐。

| **right now** | **Please finish your homework right now.** |
| *ph.* 現在 | → 請立刻完成你的作業。 |

| **no longer** | **Sarah is no longer a police .** |
| *ph.* 不再 | → 莎拉不再是警察了。 |

• •

 一定要會的萬用句

① Have you ever knitted anything before?

→ 你以前編織過任何東西嗎？

② No, never. → 從來沒有。

③ It's really "in" right now. → 它現在很流行。

④ I can't agree with you more. → 完全同意。

😎 我們也能這樣說

① I've definitely decided to go to college in California.

→ 我已經確定要去加州唸大學了。

② Have you ever seen that movie before?

→ 你以前曾看過那部電影嗎？

③ Have you ever been to Europe?

→ 你曾經去過歐洲嗎？

④ Work takes up most of my time.

→ 工作佔掉我大部分的時間。

⑤ I'd like to take up the challenge.

→ 我願意接受挑戰。

常見錯誤不要犯

in和on是容易混淆的兩個單字，因此一不注意就可能就會說出 "It's really "on" right now." 這樣錯誤的句子。

正確的說法是 "It's really "in" right now."

介係詞 on，意為「在……上」；in 作為介係詞，當「在……裡」講。但是不同的是 in 還有個形容詞詞性，意為「時髦的」。根據句意，此處應為使用 in 而不是 on。

常見句型一起學

★ 我已經決定要做……

I've   decided   to take up knitting.

I've   decided   +   to do

I've decided... 是「我已經決定要做……事」，是現在完成式的用法。如上述會話中的 I've decided to take up knitting. 意為「我決定要學編織了。」又如 I've decided to leave the city.「我已經決定要離開這座城市了。」

以下是其他的相關例句：

▶ **I've decided to learn how to knit.**
→ 我決定要學編織了。

▶ **I've decided not to tell Timmy where his wife is.**
→ 我已經決定不告訴提米，他的老婆在哪裡。

▶ **As most of you know, I've decided to resign.**
→ 你們大都已經知道，我決定辭職了。

▶ **I believe you've decided to go home immediately.**
→ 我想你已經決定立刻回家了。

▶ **I assume you've decided to buy a new car.**
→ 我想你已經決定買輛新車了。

25 我愛死電視了

 Track 25

和朋友在聊興趣相關的事時，很容易因為彼此感興趣的事情不同而略有摩擦。我們要尊重彼此的喜好，若不想參與對方的興趣，也可以直接拒絕，避免產生更多尷尬。

A: There's nothing good on TV anymore!	最近的電視都很難看。
B: What are you talking about? I just love TV!	你在開玩笑吧！我愛死電視了。
A: It's all "reality shows" now.	現在全都是「實境秀」。
B: Those are the best!	實境秀是最棒的！
A: They're not even spontaneous. They're all staged you know.	它們不是自然演出，全都是假的，你知道吧。
B: Well, I don't care! It's good entertainment.	嗯，我不在乎，反正娛樂性很夠。
A: Count me out!	別找我一起看。

 關鍵單字要認得

anymore *adv.* 再、更	**He doesn't want to watch horror movies anymore.** → 他不想再看任何恐怖片了。
reality show *ph.* 實境秀	**Reality shows are always fun.** → 實境秀總是很有趣。

spontaneous _adj._ 自發性的	**Students in her class are spontaneous.** → 學生在她的課堂上很有自發性。
entertainment _n._ 娛樂	**I'm bored. Do you know some good entertainment?** → 我很無聊。你知道任何好娛樂嗎？
count me out _ph._ 不把……考慮在內	**I hate hiking. Please count me out.** → 我痛恨健行。請不要把我算在內。

 一定要會的萬用句

① Those are the best! → 那些是最棒的！

② They're all staged. → 全都是假的。

③ It's good entertainment. → 娛樂性很夠。

④ Count me out! → 別算我的。

 我們也能這樣說

① Can you tell me what you are doing now?

→ 你能告訴我你現在做什麼嗎？

② There's a great show at 10 on channel 39 tonight. Don't miss it.

→ 今晚十點在 39 台有個很好看的節目。別錯過喔。

③ I missed the last episode, and I'm going to watch a rerun later.

→ 我沒看到最後一集，所以待會要來看重播。

④ I'll take a rain check.

→ 下次吧。

⑤ Count me in.

→ 算我一份。

常見錯誤不要犯

介係詞的使用在英文中是非常重要的，使用不同的介係詞就會產生不同的意思，如 "Count me on!" 與 "Count me out!" 截然不同。

片語 count on 意為「依靠、指望」，相當於 depend on。片語 count out 意為「逐一數出；不把……算入」。二者意思不同，切勿混淆。

常見句型一起學

★ 現在進行式

What　　are　　you　　talking about?

疑問詞　+　be動詞　+　主詞　+　　　doing

What are you talking about! 意為「你在說什麼！」，「be＋doing」是典型的現在進行式的用法，例如：

▶ **Children are doing their homework.**
→ 孩子們正在做作業。

現在進行式的時間標誌通常有：now、right now、at the moment 等。

以下是其他的相關例句：

▶ **I am handling a big project.**
→ 我正負責一個大型專案。

▶ **Those boys are playing basketball now.**
→ 那些男孩正在打籃球。

▶ **Is she playing the piano?**
→ 她正在彈鋼琴嗎？

▶ **The farmers are gathering their crops.**
→ 農民正在收割莊稼。

▶ **They are having class at the moment.**
→ 他們正在上課。

26 我昨天加入攀岩社

 情境對話　∩ Track 26

培養良好的運動習慣是很重要的，可以邀請親朋好友一起來運動，也可以從有不同運動習慣的朋友身上瞭解到不同運動的樂趣與需要注意的事情。

A: Hi! What did you do yesterday?	嗨！你昨天做了些什麼嗎？
B: I just joined a rock climbing club yesterday.	我昨天加入了攀岩社。
A: Really? I thought you were afraid of heights.	真的嗎？我還以為妳有懼高症耶。
B: No, my sister is. I am excited about that.	不，是我姊姊才有。攀岩讓我感到興奮。
A: Good for you! How often do you go?	真好。你多久去一次呢？
B: Every Sunday. But I'm thinking of going Saturday as well. Do you want to try climbing?	每個禮拜天，但我正在考慮要不要連禮拜六也去。你想不想試試看攀岩呢？
A: Hmmm...No, I think I'll keep my feet on the ground.	嗯……不用了。我想我還是乖乖的走路就好。

 關鍵單字要認得

join
☑ 加入

Do you want to join a rock climbing club?
→ 你想加入攀岩社嗎？

be afraid of *ph.* 害怕	**My little sister is afraid of dogs.** → 我妹妹會害怕狗。
height *n.* 高度	**The height of the mountain is around 13,000 feet .** → 那座山的高度大約有13,000英呎。
sister *n.* 姊妹	**John has two sisters.** → 約翰有兩位姊妹。
on the ground *ph.* 在地上	**The box is on the ground.** → 箱子在地上。

 一定要會的萬用句

❶ What did you do yesterday? → 你昨天做了些什麼嗎？

❷ I thought you were afraid of heights.

→ 我還以為你有懼高症耶。

❸ Good for you! → 真好！

❹ I think I'll keep my feet on the ground.

→ 我想我還是乖乖的走路就好。

 我們也能這樣說

❶ I can't believe that you go rock climbing!

→ 我真的無法相信你會去攀岩！

❷ James and I went bungee jumping last weekend.

→ 我和詹姆士上週末去高空彈跳。

❸ Only a coward would run from danger. → 只有懦夫才臨陣脫逃。

❹ We thought he was a nice guy, but he isn't.

→ 我們還以為他是個好人，但卻非如此。

常見錯誤不要犯

在說英文時，要注意句型需不需要使用人稱代名詞，要小心別說出 "Why don't join us?" 這樣錯誤的句子。

正確的說法是 "Why don't you join us?"

表達「為什麼不……」可以說：why not... 或者 why don't...。當用 why not 的時候後面不需要接人稱代名詞，有 don't 的時候才加人稱代名詞。

常見句型一起學

★ 我已經決定要做……

How often　　　do　　　you go?

How often ＋ 助動詞／be動詞 ＋ 其他

表達頻率時一定會用到 How often，這類問句的回答通常會有：once a week（一週一次）、twice a day（一天兩次）、four times a year（一年四次）等。

以下是其他的相關例句：

▶ **How often do I have to take this medicine?**
→ 我必須多久吃一次藥？

▶ **How often do you have the flights to Bonn?**
→ 去波昂的飛機每隔多久會有一班？

▶ **How often does she go shopping?**
→ 她多久逛一次街？

▶ **How often do the buses run?**
→ 公車隔多久會有一班？

▶ **"How often do you go there?" "Once a month."**
→ 「你多久去那裡一次？」「一個月一次。」

27 我得找份新工作

遇上了難過的事，想要向朋友訴苦、散心的時候，若朋友卻剛好沒空，不能一起出去走走，也可以試著透過網路找人聊聊，來抒發心中的鬱悶。

A: You don't look well. What's up?	你看起來不太好哦。怎麼了？
B: I have to find a new job!	我得找份新工作！
A: You don't like where you are?	為什麼？你不喜歡現在的工作嗎？
B: No, not a bit. I'm not motivated at all.	一點都不。我一點動力都沒有。
A: Would you stay in the same field or look for something different?	你會待在相同的領域還是轉換跑道？
B: Oh...I have no idea.	噢⋯⋯我不知道。
A: When are you going to start looking?	那你哪時候會開始找工作呢？
B: Oh...I don't know, either. I can't get motivated!	噢⋯⋯我也不知道。我還沒有動力！

關鍵單字要認得

a bit
ph. 一點

It didn't hurt a bit when the baby hit me.
→ 小嬰兒打我的時候一點也不痛。

motivate
☑ 激發

He was motivated by fear.
→ 恐懼激發他的動力。

look for
ph. 尋找

I'm looking for Harry.
→ 我在尋找哈利。

different
adj 不同的

The two books are different.
→ 兩本書不一樣。

- -

 一定要會的萬用句

❶ You don't look well.

　→ 你看起來不太好哦。

❷ You don't like where you are?

　→ 你不喜歡現在的工作嗎？

❸ No, not a bit. → 一點都不。

❹ I can't get motivated! → 我沒有動力。

 我們也能這樣說

❶ Not in any way.

　→ 一點都不。

❷ I have to look for a new job!

　→ 我得找份新工作。

❸ You will find it difficult to deal with.

　→ 你會發現它很難處理。

❹ I don't like the atmosphere there.

　→ 我不喜歡那裡的氣氛。

常見錯誤不要犯

在說英文時，要注意不是意思相似的詞都能通用，如 "Not a little." 和 "Not a bit." 就是兩個極為相似又極容易混淆的片語。not a little 意為「不是一點兒、不少、很多」；而 not a bit 意為「一點也不、絲毫不」。可見二者意思完全不同，一定要注意區分。

 常見句型一起學

★ 表達將要做某事

When   are you going to start looking?

疑問詞　＋　　　　　be going to do

表達將要做某事，除了用 will do 之外，還可以用 be going to do，兩者都是未來式。

以下是其他的相關例句：

▶ **Accidents will happen.**
→ 世事難料。

▶ **Will Friday do?**
→ 星期五可以嗎？

▶ **Who is he going to show pictures to?**
→ 他要把照片給誰看？

▶ **He is going to Canada to seek his fortune.**
→ 他想去加拿大賺大錢。

▶ **He is going to report them to the police.**
→ 他打算向警方告發他們。

28 我討厭我的生活

 情境對話 🎧 Track 28

在向朋友抱怨生活中不順心的事時，可能朋友也有相似的困境，甚至還比自己更不好過，在抱怨的時候要注意別在對方的傷口上灑鹽。每個人都會在生活中碰到糟心的事，希望能找到好方法來排解煩悶。

A: What's bothering you?	你在煩什麼啊？
B: I hate my life!	我討厭我的生活！
A: Hate your life? But I think you have it made.	討厭你的生活？我覺得你過得蠻好的呀！
B: Have it made? How would you like to take a million tests every week? When I'm not taking tests, I'm studying!	過得蠻好的？你喜歡每個禮拜都有考不完的試嗎？我如果不是在考試就是在唸書。
A: OK, how would you like to pay a million bills every week? And when I'm not paying bills, I'm looking after everyone in the family!	好，那你喜歡每個禮拜都有付不完的帳單嗎？還有，我如果不是在付帳單就是在照顧家裡的每一個人。
B: Yeah, OK. You made your point!	好啦，好啦。我知道你的意思了！

 關鍵單字要認得

hate
🔲 憎恨、討厭

I hate doing homework.
→ 我痛恨寫作業。

million *n.* 百萬	**There are millions of people waiting for the new episode of the show.** → 有百萬人在等待新一集的電視劇。
test *n.* 測試	**Harry has a test tomorrow.** → 哈利明天有個考試。
every week *ph.* 每週	**May buys a book every week.** → 梅每個禮拜都會買一本書。
look after *ph.* 照顧	**David will look after his sister.** → 大衛會照顧他的妹妹。
made your point *ph.* 講出關鍵性的重點	**You have made your point loud and clear.** → 你把關鍵性的重點說得很清楚明瞭了。

• •

 一定要會的萬用句

❶ What's bothering you? → 你在煩什麼啊？

❷ I hate my life! → 我討厭我的生活！

❸ I'm looking after everyone in the family! → 我照顧家裡的每一個人！

❹ You made your point! → 我知道你的意思了！

 我們也能這樣說

❶ I think you have a good life. → 我覺得你的生活過得蠻不錯的。

❷ Tom didn't like his school life at all. → 湯姆一點也不喜歡學校生活。

❸ Nina and David couldn't stand the noise.

→ 妮娜和大衛受不了那些噪音。

❹ Many people enjoy playing online games. → 很多人喜歡玩線上遊戲。

❺ Does your kid like going to school? → 你的小孩喜歡上學嗎？

常見錯誤不要犯

若想用英文表達「重點、關鍵」的意思,可能會想到key這個單字,因此說出 "You made your key!" 這樣錯誤的句子。

正確的說法是 "You made your point!"。

片語 make one's point 意為「講出某人關鍵性的重點」。key 雖然有「關鍵」的意思,但在此片語中不可以隨意替換。

常見句型一起學

★ 表達內心的想法

I think you have it made.

I   think +   (that) 子句

直接表達某人內心的想法,可以用這個句型。除了 think 之外,還可以用 believe,如 I believe your dream will come true one day.(我相信你的夢想有一天會實現。)

以下是其他的相關例句:

▶ **I think your explanation is right.**
→ 我認為你的說明很正確。

▶ **I think I have no other choice.**
→ 我想我別無選擇。

▶ **I think I have overlooked that point.**
→ 我想我忽視了這一點。

▶ **I believe he is innocent.**
→ 我相信他是無辜的。

▶ **I believe the answer is wrong.**
→ 我堅信答案是錯誤的。

29 這個週末打算做什麼

和朋友共享快樂的時光向來是生活中相當重要的一部分，除了聊天之外，也能一起玩線上遊戲、看電影、討論音樂等。

A: What are you planning to do this weekend?	你這個週末打算做什麼？
B: I have no idea. What about you?	不知道哎。你呢？
A: Let's actually do something this weekend! It would be nice to get out!	我們這週末來做些事吧！出去走走也不錯！
B: Like what?	比如説？
A: I don't know. Watch a movie?	我不知道。看電影好嗎？
B: What's playing?	現在正在上映哪些電影呢？
A: Lots of good ones. I'll check online.	有很多好看的電影啊。我上網查。

 關鍵單字要認得

plan	**I plan to go to the shopping mall this Sunday.**
v. 計劃	→ 這個星期天我打算去購物中心。
watch a movie	**We can watch a movie together.**
ph. 看電影	→ 我們可以一起看電影。

lots of	**There are lots if people in the school.**
ph. 許多	→ 學校裡有很多人。

check	**I'll check my schedule first.**
v. 檢查	→ 我會先確認我的行程表。

- -

 一定要會的萬用句

① Like what? → 比如説？

② Catch a movie? → 看電影好嗎？

③ What's playing?

→ 現在正在上映哪些電影呢？

④ It would be nice to get out!

→ 出去走走也不錯！

 我們也能這樣說

① Anything you'd like to do for the weekend?

→ 你這個週末有想要做的事嗎？

② Do you have any plans for the coming weekend?

→ 你這個週末有任何計劃嗎？

③ I don't feel like going anywhere.

→ 我哪裡都不想去。

④ Let's stay home instead of going out.

→ 我們待在家裡不要出門吧！

⑤ It would be nice to travel there!

→ 去那裡旅行一定很棒！

表達「看電影」有很多不同的説法，除了watch a movie以外，
還可以説：see a movie 或者 go to the cinema，還可以説
catch a movie。

但是 "seize a movie" 是錯誤的説法，雖然seize 和 catch 都有
「抓住」的意思，但在此片語中不能隨意替換。

常見句型一起學

★ 表達建議

Let's   actually do something this weekend!

Let's   +   原形動詞

表達建議性的句子可以用這個句型，Let's 實際上是 Let us 的縮寫形式。

以下是其他的相關例句：

▶ **Let's compare 2000 with 2008.**
→ 請大家對比一下 2000 年和 2008 年的情況。

▶ **Let's dine out!**
→ 我們到餐廳吃飯吧！

▶ **Let's play singles!**
→ 我們來玩單打！

▶ **Let's bet on it!**
→ 我們打個賭吧！

▶ **It's 12:00. Let's go.**
→ 現在十二點了，我們走吧。

30 颱風要來了

 情境對話　∩ Track 30

在天氣變化大的地區，隨時注意天氣預報是很重要的，而若有朋友住在容易發生颱風、暴風雪等災害的地方，也可以幫他注意天氣預報喔！

A: Did you hear the weather forecast?	你有收聽氣象預報嗎？
B: No. Why?	沒有。怎麼了？
A: Well, there's a typhoon coming.	嗯，有颱風要來。
B: No way!	不會吧！
A: Yep, It should be here by tomorrow night.	沒錯，颱風應該明晚就會來。
B: Awesome! No school!	太棒了！不用去上學了！
A: I never know you hate studying so much!	我從來不知道你這麼討厭唸書啊！

 關鍵單字要認得

hear ☑ 收聽	**I can't hear what David is saying.** → 我聽不見大衛正在說什麼。
typhoon ☑ 颱風	**We have a typhoon the day after tomorrow.** → 後天會有颱風來。

no way	**There is no way she can help you.**
ph. 不可能、別想	→ 她不可能幫助你。

awesome	**This chocolate is awesome.**
adj. 棒極了	→ 這個巧克力棒極了。

• •

 一定要會的萬用句

❶ Did you hear the weather forecast?

→ 你有收聽氣象預報嗎？

❷ There's a typhoon coming.

→ 有颱風要來。

❸ No way! → 不會吧！

❹ Awesome! → 太棒了！

 我們也能這樣說

❶ What's the weather like today?

→ 今天天氣如何？

❷ Did you watch the weather forecast last night?

→ 你昨晚有看氣象報告嗎？

❸ There's a typhoon coming this way.

→ 有颱風要來。

❹ The forecast says we'll have a typhoon tomorrow.

→ 氣象報告說明天有颱風。

❺ There's a snowstorm coming.

→ 有暴風雪要來。

常見錯誤不要犯

在英文中，要注意句子裡的動詞變化，以免說出 "I never know you hate study so much!" 的錯誤用法。

正確說法是 "I never know you hate studying so much!"

hate to do sth. 意為「討厭做某事」；hate doing sth. 意為「討厭某種行為」。二者的區別在於：hate to do sth. 是指具體的一次動作；而 hate doing sth. 是一個經常性的動作。在此句中，hate 後面不能直接加動詞原形。

常見句型一起學

★ 表達建議

No　school!

No ＋ 名詞／動名詞

No school! 這是個省略句，英文解釋應為 We don't have to go to school! 意為我們不用去上學了。No後面可以接名詞，也可以接動名詞。

以下是其他的相關例句：

▶ **No Smoking.**
→ 禁止吸煙。

▶ **No reply.**
→ 沒有回應。

▶ **No signal.**
→ 沒有訊號。

▶ **No problem.**
→ 沒問題。

▶ **No way!**
→ 想都別想！

31 打算出國讀書嗎

 情境對話

出國深造能開闊眼界，上網搜尋能找到許多相關資訊喔！

A: What are you up to?	你在做什麼？
B: Nothing much, just surfing the net.	沒什麼。我在上網。
A: Anything interesting?	有沒有什麼有趣的東西呢？
B: Yeah, I found a site that has a lot of info about schools in Europe.	有呀！我找到一個有很多關於歐洲學校資料的網站。
A: Are you planning to study abroad?	你有打算出國讀書嗎？
B: Yap. I just sent a few e-mails to some schools and I think I'll download some application forms for others.	是啊。我寄了幾封電子信件給一些學校，我想我還會再下載其他學校的申請表。
A: I am so envious of you having the opportunity to study abroad.	我真羨慕你有機會出國留學。

關鍵單字要認得

surf ☑ 衝浪、瀏覽	**I surf the net every night.** → 我每天晚上都會上網。
interesting *adj.* 有趣的	**This book is interesting.** → 這本書很有趣。

102

| **send**
☑ 發送 | **Please send me the report.**
→ 請把報告寄給我。 |
| **download**
☑ 下載 | **David downloaded the social software to make friends.**
→ 大衛下載了社群軟體來交更多朋友。 |

· ·

 一定要會的萬用句

① What are you up to? → 你在做什麼？

② Nothing much. → 沒什麼。

③ Anything interesting?

    → 有沒有什麼有趣的東西呢？

④ Are you planning to study abroad?

    → 你有打算出國讀書嗎？

 我們也能這樣說

① Are you in the middle of something now?

    → 你現在在忙些什麼嗎？

② Nothing special.

    → 沒什麼。

③ I'm doing my research.

    → 我在做調查。

④ I'm in the middle of my project.

    → 我在忙著做企劃。

⑤ I sent Mr. Lee an e-mail telling him about my resignation

    → 我昨晚寄了電子郵件給李先生告知他我要辭職的事。

常見錯誤不要犯

something和anything要注意別混淆了，避免說出 "Something interesting?" 這樣的錯誤用法。

正確說法是 "Anything interesting?"

不定代詞 something 用於肯定句；anything 用於否定句和疑問句。此句為疑問句，應該使用 anything 而不是 something。

常見句型一起學

★ 詢問別人正在做什麼

What are you up to?

What + be 動詞 + 名詞 + up to V-ing?

詢問別人正在做什麼可以用這個句型，其中 up to 在此有正在做之意。也可翻譯成「你在忙什麼？」，還可以說 What are you doing?（你在幹嘛呢？）。

以下是其他的相關例句：

▶ **What's she up to?**
→ 她在忙什麼？

▶ **What are they up to recently?**
→ 他們最近在忙什麼？

▶ **What are you up to lately?**
→ 你們最近在做什麼？

▶ **What is mom doing?**
→ 媽媽在幹嘛？

▶ **Can you tell me what he is doing now?**
→ 你能告訴我他在忙什麼嗎？

32 油價還會上升

 情境對話　∩ Track 31

除了自己生活中的事情外，也可以多和朋友聊聊一些與整個社會相關的議題，如民生問題、環境議題都是很容易引起共鳴的話題，每個人都會關心油價和物價，而環境保育也是每個人都該重視的。

A: Why are you so angry?	你為什麼這麼生氣啊？
B: Can you believe the price of petroleum right now?	現在的油價真令人不可置信。
A: I know. It's shocking! When's it going to stop?	沒錯。真的太糟了！真不知這何時會停止？
B: I guess it won't unless the U.S. dollar drops.	我想除非美元貶值，否則油價還會往上升。
A: We should all protest by driving less!	我們應該少開車來表達抗議。
B: I've already started by walking more and taking the train.	我已經開始多走路並且搭火車了。
A: More people should follow your example!	更多人應以你為榜樣！
B: Yeah, and you should be the first one.	對啊，而且你應該當第一個！

 關鍵單字要認得

unless *conj.* 除非	**I will not go unless they invite me.** → 如果他們不邀請我，我就不去。

drop ☑ 貶值；落下	**Sam dropped his book.** → 山姆掉了他的書。
protest ☑ 抗議	**These people is protesting for the environment.** → 這些人正為了環境抗議。
follow ... example 效法某人	**Please follow your teacher's example.** → 請效法你老師的行為。

• •

 一定要會的萬用句

❶ Why are you so angry? → 你為什麼這麼生氣啊？

❷ When's it going to stop? → 何時會停止？

❸ We should all protest by driving less! → 我們應該少開車來表達抗議。

❹ More people should follow your example! → 更多人應以你為榜樣！

 我們也能這樣說

❶ I guess we all need to do something for our planet.

→ 我猜我們都要為地球做些什麼。

❷ More people should do the same!

→ 更多人應該這樣做！

❸ You've set a good example for others.

→ 你已經為其他人建立一個好榜樣了。

❹ Children should follow their parents' example.

→ 孩子都應該以父母親為榜樣。

❺ Can't believe he is a famous writer now!

→ 真不敢相信他現在是個著名的作家！

常見錯誤不要犯

當動詞的現在分詞和過去分詞可以作為形容詞使用時，注意別混淆了，要避免説出 "It's shocked!" 這樣的錯誤用法。

正確説法是 "It's shocking!"

現在分詞 shocking 意為「令人震驚的」；過去分詞 shocked 意為「感到震驚的」。二者的區別在於，形容「某事令人震驚」用 shocking；形容「某人感到震驚」用 shocked。

 常見句型一起學

★ 除非……否則就……

I guess it won't (stop)　unless　the U.S. dollar drops.

主句　　　　　　　　　　+　unless　+　　　其他

表達「除非……否則就……」可以用 unless 句型，相當於 if not。

以下是其他的相關例句：

▶ **You'll lag behind unless you study harder.**
→ 你如果不更加努力地學習，就會落後。

▷ **Talent is worthless unless you develop it.**
→ 除非你好好發展，否則天賦本身沒有價值。

▶ **I will not go unless I hear from him.**
→ 如果他不通知我，我就不去。

▷ **It is easily forgotten unless constantly repeated.**
→ 除非不斷重複，否則很容易忘記。

▶ **He will kill her if we can't prevent him.**
→ 如果我們不阻止他，他就會殺了她。

33 全世界到處旅行的工作

 情境對話 　∩ Track 32

透過網路，可以認識各式各樣的人，不同國家的網友可以介紹不同國家的文化，從事不同工作的網友也能聊聊自己工作的快樂和辛酸，網路可以讓我們更認識這個世界。

A: You have a pretty sweet job that you can travel around the world.	你有份很棒的工作，能在全世界到處旅行。
B: Well, there are a few little drawbacks though, to living out of a suitcase.	嗯，提著行李到處生活還是有些小缺點啦。
A: Like what?	比如說？
B: Ummm... sometimes I'm only in a city for a few hours, then I have to move on to the next one.	嗯……有時我只在一個城市待幾個小時，然後就得到下個城市。
A: At least you're in another city.	至少你還在另外一個城市。
B: Yeah, I know, but I can also get really sick from the food.	沒錯，我知道，但有時我也會因吃錯食物而生病。
A: Oh, that's not too good. Take good care of yourself.	噢，那可不太好。要好好照顧自己哦。

 關鍵單字要認得

pretty
adv. 相當

I pretty like the design of the book.
→ 我很喜歡這本書的設計。

suitcase *n.* 手提箱	**Sam has a suitcase full of books.** → 山姆有一個裝滿書的手提箱。
at least *ph.* 至少	**You have to wait at least one hour.** → 你至少需要等一個小時。
get sick *ph.* 生病	**Tom got sick yesterday.** → 湯姆昨天生病了。

• •

 一定要會的萬用句

❶ You have a pretty sweet job. → 你有份很棒的工作。

❷ There are a few little drawbacks though.

→ 還是有些小缺點啦。

❸ Like what? → 比如說？

❹ Oh, that's not too good. → 噢，那可不太好。

😎 我們也能這樣說

❶ I've got an incredible job.

→ 我有份超讚的工作。

❷ Diana has a decent job.

→ 戴安娜有一份正當的工作。

❸ Karen's got a low-paying job.

→ 凱倫有份待遇很低的工作。

❹ Would you like to exchange jobs?

→ 要交換工作嗎？

❺ Jim eventually decided to quit.

→ 吉姆最終決定辭掉他的工作。

 常見句型一起學

★ 表達轉折

There are a few little drawbacks　　though.

句子　　　　　　　　　　　　　+　　　though

表達轉折的句子除了會用到 but，though 也是一個常用的詞，意為雖然、儘管，可
以置於句首或者句尾。

以下是其他的相關例句：

▶ **Though he was angry, he listened to me patiently.**
→ 他雖生氣，但他耐心聽我說。

▶ **Though we lost our money, we learned our lesson.**
→ 雖然丟了錢，但我們得了教訓。

▶ **Though naughty, my children are quite lovely.**
→ 雖然我的孩子很頑皮，但可愛。

▶ **The salary was inadequate, David accepted the position
though.**
→ 雖然薪水不高，大衛還是接受了聘任。

▶ **I am hardworking, though I am not clever.**
→ 雖然我不聰明，但很努力。

34 你是做什麼工作的

若認識從事各行各業的人，可以多聽他們聊不同行業的甘苦談，也可以跟對方分享與自己的行業或生活相關的事情。

A: Nice to meet you, Melisa.	梅莉莎，見到妳很高興。
B: Nice to meet you, too. So, what do you do?	我也很高興見到你。那麼，你是做什麼工作的？
A: I'm a firefighter.	我是消防員。
B: Really? That's so cool.	真的嗎？真酷。
A: Ha, ha. I'm pretty lucky to do something I really love.	哈哈。我真的相當幸運能做我喜愛的事。
B: What station do you work at?	你在哪個消防局工作呢？
A: I work at station 24. It can get a little crazy sometimes but that's what makes it challenging.	我在 24 分局工作。這個工作有時有些瘋狂，但這也是它很具挑戰性的原因。

關鍵單字要認得

firefighter
⤵ 消防員

He is proud of his son who is a firefighter.
→ 他為他在當消防員的兒子感到很驕傲。

cool *adj.* 酷	**This movie is so cool.** → 這個電影非常酷。
lucky *adj.* 幸運的	**I was so lucky that I won the lottery.** → 我能中樂透真是太幸運了。
station *n.* （機構的）局、站	**Tom is waiting at the bus station.** → 湯姆在公車站等待。
work at *ph.* 在……工作	**David works at the global company.** → 大衛在那間跨國公司工作。

• •

 一定要會的萬用句

① What do you do? → 你是做什麼工作的？

② I'm a firefighter. → 我是消防員。

③ I'm pretty lucky to do something I really love.

→ 我真的相當幸運能做我喜愛的事。

④ It can get a little crazy sometimes but that's what makes it challenging.

→ 這個工作有時有些瘋狂，但這也是為何這個工作很具挑戰性的原因。

 我們也能這樣說

① What do you do to make a living? → 你靠什麼過活？

② We just do our best. → 我們只是盡全力去做。

③ We just do our part. → 我們只是盡本分。

④ We never complain. → 我們從不抱怨。

⑤ I am always busy at work, but I enjoy it anyway.

→ 我總是忙於工作，但我還是很喜歡。

常見錯誤不要犯

either 和 too 都有「也」的意思，容易搞混，譬如說 "Nice to meet you, either." 是錯誤的說法。

正確說法是 "Nice to meet you, too."

either 和 too的區別在於：either 用於否定句，而 too 用於肯定句。
另外，too 用在句尾時，句子與 too 要用逗號隔開；either 用在
否定句中時, 句子與 either 之間也要用逗號隔開。

常見句型一起學

★ 助動詞與謂語動詞

What　do　you　do?

What + 助動詞 + 主詞 + 其他

詢問他人的職業可以說 what do you do? 其中第一個 do 為助動詞，用來提問，第二個 do 才是句子的謂語動詞，意為「做」。與之類似的如 I had had it before last year.（我去年就有它了。）句子中的第一個 had 是過去完成時的標誌，沒有實際意義，第二個 had 就是實意動詞擁有。

以下是其他的相關例句：

▶ **What's her occupation?**
→ 她是做什麼的？

▶ **What does your father do?**
→ 你父親是做什麼的？

▶ **What's your job?**
→ 你做什麼工作？

▶ **What do they do at present?**
→ 他們目前在做些什麼？

▶ **What do you do for a living?**
→ 你從事什麼工作？

35 恭喜你搬進新房子

 情境對話　∩ Track 34

喬遷可說是人生大事之一，當朋友想要搬家的時候，可以對朋友選擇的地段、裝潢等提供意見，除此之外，一定要好好肯定對方對買房子做出的努力。

A: Congratulations on the new house!	恭喜你搬進了新房子！
B: Thanks! I love it.	謝謝！我很喜歡。
A: Well, you worked hard for it. It's really beautiful.	嗯……你為了這間房子真的很努力。房子非常漂亮。
B: I'm just not looking forward to cleaning it!	倒是我非常不願意去想到打掃房子的問題！
A: Come on! I am so jealous of you!	少來了！我都嫉妒你了！
B: Don't worry! I believe you can buy one soon.	別擔心。我相信很快你也能買一棟的。

 關鍵單字要認得

work hard *ph.* 努力工作	**He worked hard for a new car.** → 他為了新車很努力工作。
beautiful *adj.* 漂亮的	**This skirt is very beautiful.** → 這件裙子非常漂亮。
look forward to *ph.* 期待	**I am looking forward to going shopping.** → 我很期待去購物。

jealous

 adj. 嫉妒的

Sam is jealous of you because you won the lottery.

→ 山姆因為你中樂透而嫉妒你。

- -

 一定要會的萬用句

① Congratulations on the new house!

→ 恭喜你搬進了新房子！

② You guys worked hard for it.

→ 你們為了這個真的很努力。

③ Come on!

→ 少來了！

④ I am so jealous of you!

→ 我都嫉妒你了！

😎 我們也能這樣說

① She'll pass your blessing to them.

→ 她會傳達你的祝福給他們的。

② I'll deliver the best wishes to them for you.

→ 我會為你傳達祝賀給他們的。

③ I really appreciate that.

→ 我很感激。

④ How nice of you!

→ 你人真好。

常見句型一起學

★ 表達祝賀某人某事

Congratulations on   the new house!

Congratulations on   +   名詞

直接表達祝賀某人某事的時候可以用Congratulations on。

以下是其他的相關例句：

▶ **Congratulations on your wedding.**
→ 恭賀新婚之喜。

▷ **Congratulations on the graduation!**
→ 恭喜畢業了！

▶ **Congratulations on your birthday.**
→ 恭賀生日快樂。

▷ **Congratulations on the century celebration.**
→ 恭賀世紀慶典。

▶ **Congratulations on your ten-year anniversary of marriage.**
→ 恭喜結婚十週年快樂。

36 我感到很遺憾

當與朋友失聯時，不禁擔心對方的狀況，等到再見到他時，可以關心對方發生了什麼事。

A: Haven't seen you for days. Where have you been?	好幾天沒看到你了。你去哪兒了？
B: My father passed away last week.	我父親上個禮拜去世了。
A: I'm so sorry about your dad.	對於你爸爸的事我感到很遺憾。
B: Thank you.	謝謝。
A: Is there anything I can do for you and your family?	有什麼事我可以幫忙你或你家人的嗎？
B: No, thanks. My mom's making all the arrangements right now.	沒有，謝謝你。我媽媽籌備了一切事宜。
A: All right, call me for anything, even if it's just to talk.	好吧，任何時候都可以打給我，即使只想聊聊。
B: I appreciate that so much.	我真的很感激。

 關鍵單字要認得

anything
pron. 任何東西

Tom can do anything for his girlfriend.
→ 湯姆可以為了他的女朋友做任何事。

family
n. 家庭

May needs to look after her family.
→ 梅必須照顧她的家庭。

arrangement
n. 安排

She will make all the arrangements for the party.
→ 她會籌備好派對的相關事宜。

appreciate
v. 感激

I appreciate all the help you gave me during this year.
→ 我感激你這一年來的協助。

 一定要會的萬用句

❶ Haven't seen you for days. → 好幾天沒看到你了。

❷ Is there anything I can do for you and your family?
→ 有什麼事我可以幫忙你或你家的嗎？

❸ My mom's making all the arrangements right now.
→ 我媽媽籌備了一切事宜。

❹ I appreciate that so much. → 我真的很感激。

 我們也能這樣說

❶ Please accept my condolences. → 請接受我的慰問。

❷ I would like to express my condolences about your dad.
→ 我想表達對你父親的弔唁。

❸ Can you do me a favor? → 你能幫我個忙嗎？

❹ Funeral customs vary with different religions.
→ 葬禮的習俗因宗教差異而不同。

❺ I see. Call me for anything. → 我瞭解，隨時都能打給我。

❻ He will come on time even though it's raining.
→ 即使下雨，他還是會準時來的。

常見錯誤不要犯

有時候即使文法正確了，但句子仍然要避免使用，如 "My father died last week." 就是不能使用的說法。

正確說法是 "My father passed away last week."

片語 pass away 是表達「死」的一種非常委婉的表達方式，意為「去世、過世」。這個句子本身文法沒有錯誤，die 的確是「死」的意思，但是表達上過於直接生硬，也是對於逝者的不尊重。

常見句型一起學

★ 遺憾、惋惜

I'm so sorry   about   your dad.

I'm so sorry   about／for + 名詞／doing

表達對某事感到抱歉或者遺憾、惋惜可以用這個句型。

以下是其他的相關例句：

▶ **I'm sorry about causing you so much trouble!**
→ 給你添了這麼多麻煩真抱歉！

▶ **I feel sorry for keeping you waiting.**
→ 讓你等待我感到很抱歉。

▶ **I'm so sorry about your mother's passing away.**
→ 對於你母親的過世我感到很遺憾。

▶ **I'm sorry for hearing that you failed in the exam.**
→ 聽說你考試沒過我感到惋惜。

▶ **I'm so sorry about losing such an important client.**
→ 失去了這麼重要的客戶我感到很可惜。

37 新年祝福

 情境對話　∩ Track 36

新年倒數是在全球各地都會有的慶祝活動，可以趁著這個時間，和親朋好友們一起度過，省思一年來的收穫，也展望未來。

A: 5-4-3-2-1! Happy New Year!	5、4、3、2、1，新年快樂！
B: Happy New Year! Here's to a great year! Cheers!	新年快樂！祝有美好的一年！乾杯！
A: Cheers! Yeah, let's hope it's better than last year.	乾杯！是啊，希望今年會比去年好。
B: Here's to getting rich this year.	祝你今年賺大錢。
A: I'll drink to that!	為此乾一杯！
B: Let's drink to everything good!	讓我們為一切美好乾杯！

 關鍵單字要認得

cheers　☑ 歡呼、喝彩、乾杯	**Here's to the happy life of newlyweds! Cheers!**　→ 為了新婚夫妻的快樂生活乾杯！
hope　☑ 希望	**I hope that we can both pass the test.**　→ 我希望我們都可以通過考試。

better than	**This book is better than that one.**
ph. 更好	→ 這本書比那本更好。

last year	**We celebrated Christmas together last year .**
ph. 去年	→ 我們去年一起慶祝聖誕節。

 一定要會的萬用句

❶ Happy New Year!

→ 新年快樂！

❷ Here's to a great year!

→ 祝你有美好的一年！

❸ Cheers! → 乾杯！

❹ I'll drink to that!

→ 為此乾一杯！

 我們也能這樣說

❶ I see eye to eye with you.

→ 我同意你的說法。

❷ That sounds great!

→ 聽起來很棒！（表示同意對方）

❸ Nothing is worse than war.

→ 沒有什麼比戰爭更糟的。

❹ This one is the bigger one of the two houses.

→ 這所房子是兩座房子中較大的。

要比較兩個物件的優劣時，會用到比較級，若說一個東西是最好的，則需要用到最高級。要注意在比較的時候要避免誤用，如 "Let's hope it's best than last year." 就是錯誤的說法。

正確說法是 "Let's hope it's better than last year."

better 是 good / well 的比較級形式；best 是 good / well 的最高級形式。這裡是比較今年和去年，因此須使用比較級。

常見句型一起學

★ 表達祝福

Here's to a great year!

Here's + to + 名詞

Here's to getting rich this year.

Here's + to + 動名詞

表達美好祝福的時候，可以用這個句型，後面既可以直接加名詞，也可以用 doing 的形式來表示。以下是其他的相關例句：

▶ **Here's to a new starting.**
→ 祝你有個新的開始。

▶ **Here's to a happy ending.**
→ 祝你們有個好結局。

▶ **Here's to making more money!**
→ 祝你們賺更多的錢。

▶ **Here's to getting more beautiful.**
→ 祝你越來越漂亮。

▶ **Here's to having a harvest year.**
→ 祝你有個豐收的一年。

38 情人節要做什麼

 情境對話 🎧 **Track 37**

情人節的這一天是眾多情侶希望能共同度過、慶祝的日子，想要和伴侶度過值得紀念的一天的話，可以提早規劃，若是不希望被伴侶知道自己的秘密計畫，也可以考慮透過網路和朋友商量喔。

A: What are you and Corey doing for Valentine's Day this Friday?	妳和柯瑞這星期五情人節要做什麼？
B: Probably nothing.	可能什麼也不做。
A: You have to do something romantic.	妳應該做些浪漫的事。
B: Romantic? I can't remember what that word means!	浪漫？我都不記得那字是什麼意思了！
A: Well, you have three kids, so you should know what it meant once upon a time!	嗯……妳有三個孩子了，所以在很久以前妳是應該知道的！
B: Ha, ha! Those days are long gone.	哈哈哈！那些日子都過去很久了。
A: I know. Romance becomes waste in marriage life.	我知道。浪漫在婚姻生活裡就變成浪費了。

 關鍵單字要認得

Valentine's Day
ph. 情人節

What are you going to do on Valentine's Day?
→ 情人節你們打算做什麼？

probably *adv.* 可能	**He probably forgot the test.** → 他可能忘記考試了。
romantic *adj.* 浪漫的	**David loves to watch romantic movies .** → 大衛喜歡看愛情片。
remember *v.* 記得	**Do you remember to do the laundry?** → 你有記得洗衣服嗎？
once upon a time *ph.* 很久以前	**Once upon a time there was a princess living in a castle .** → 很久以前，有一位公主住在城堡裡。

● ●

 一定要會的萬用句

❶ Probably nothing.　→ 可能什麼也不做。

❷ You have to do something romantic.　→ 你應該做些浪漫的事。

❸ I can't remember what that word means!

　　→ 我都不記得那字是什麼意思了！

❹ Those days are long gone.　→ 那些日子都過去很久了。

 我們也能這樣說

❶ Try something interesting and romantic on Valentine's Day.

　　→ 試著在情人節那天做一些有趣浪漫的事。

❷ I did those romantic things in the old days.

　　→ 那些浪漫的事是我很久以前做過的。

❸ Those days are over.　→ 那些日子已經過去了。

❹ It is a gone case.　→ 那是一件無可挽回的事。

❺ I haven't seen you for ages.　→ 我很久沒看到你了！

常見錯誤不要犯

當疑問句被放在子句中時，句型結構會和普通的疑問句不同，如
"I can't remember what does that word mean!" 是錯誤的說法。

正確說法是 "I can't remember what that word means!"

這個句型屬於名詞子句。名詞子句的子句是疑問句的時候，疑問語序
應該變為陳述語序。在此句中，不能用 what does that word mean
而應該是 what that word means。

👍 常見句型一起學

★ 表達事物已經消失不見

Those days   are   long gone.

名詞   + be動詞／助動詞 + 過去分詞

表達什麼事物已經消失不見可以用這個句型，其中 gone 意為過去、消失、不見。

以下是其他的相關例句：

▶ **All my stuff in the room has gone.**
→ 我房間的東西都不見了。

▶ **Gone with the wind.**
→ 隨風飄逝。

▶ **Are your memories all gone?**
→ 你完全失憶了嗎？

▶ **That magician was gone within seconds.**
→ 那個魔術師在幾秒內就消失了。

▶ **Let bygones be bygones.**
→ 過去就過去吧。

39 你喜歡壽司和生魚片嗎

 情境對話 ∩ Track 38

不同的國家有不同的飲食文化，可以透過網路認識不同國家的朋友之後，請他們介紹當地的特色美食，有朝一日也能自己親自去試試看喔。

A: Do you like Sushi and Sashimi?	你喜歡吃壽司和生魚片嗎？
B: I heard about Sushi and Sashimi a long time ago. But I've never tried one.	我好久之前就聽說過壽司和生魚片了。但是從沒吃過。
A: Yesterday, people told me Japan's fishing industry is prosperous. That might be why Japanese eat Sushi and Sashimi.	昨天人們告訴我日本的漁業很發達。我想這就是為什麼日本人會吃壽司和生魚片吧。
B: Sounds reasonable! Maybe it deserves its reputation.	有道理！或許它名不虛傳。

 關鍵單字要認得

hear about *ph.* 聽說	**I have heard about the horror movie.** → 我有聽說過那部恐怖片。
a long time ago *ph.* 很久以前	**I left the city a long time ago.** → 我很久以前就離開城市了。
industry *n.* 工業	**The tourist industry here is prosperous.** → 這裡的旅遊業很發達。

126

deserve its reputation

ph. 名不虛傳

Chocolate of Belgium deserves its reputation.
→ 比利時的巧克力名不虛傳。

 一定要會的萬用句

❶ I heard about Sushi and Sashimi a long time ago.
→ 我好久之前就聽說過壽司和生魚片了。

❷ I've never tried it. → 從沒試過。

❸ That might be why Japanese eat Sushi and Sashimi.
→ 我想這就是為什麼日本人會吃壽司和生魚片吧。

❹ Sounds reasonable! → 有道理！

❺ It deserves its reputation.
→ 它名不虛傳。

 我們也能這樣說

❶ Have you eaten the pizza here?
→ 你吃過這的披薩嗎？

❷ What is today's special?
→ 今天的特餐是什麼啊？

❸ Can I try the food on the table?
→ 我能嚐嚐桌上的食物嗎？

❹ Do you need me to serve the wine now?
→ 需要先為您上酒嗎？

❺ This dish is very delicious!
→ 這道菜很美味！

句子中的動詞要如何變化是學習英文的重點之一，要避免 "Do you like eat Sushi and Sashimi?" 的錯誤說法。

正確說法是 "Do you like eating Sushi and Sashimi?"

like 的用法是 like to do 或者 like doing，並沒有 like 直接加動詞原形的用法。like to do 或者 like doing 的區別是：like to do 一般表示的是偶爾一次的動作；而 like doing 一般表示愛好。

常見句型一起學

★ 這就是為什麼……

That might be why　Japanese　eats　Sushi and Sashimi.

That's why　+　主詞　+　動詞 +　　　　　受詞

That's why＋主詞＋動詞＋受詞，這個句型的意思是「這就是為什麼……」，或者是「這就是……的原因」，用來解釋一種現象或事件。

以下是其他的相關例句：

▶ **That's why he never married.**
→ 這就是為什麼他不結婚。

▷ **That's why we came and consulted you.**
→ 因此，我們才去徵求你的意見。

▶ **That's why they decided to revise the plan.**
→ 這就是他們為什麼決定要修改計畫。

▷ **That's why I'd like to make a copy of it.**
→ 這就是為什麼我想複製一份。

40 休假要做什麼

休假是該好好放鬆的時刻，無論是想休息、趁機整理房間或出去旅行，都可以趁這個時間做。不知道該怎麼規劃的話，也可以跟朋友討論看看。

A: What do you want to do tomorrow? I have to clean my room. It's a mess.	你明天打算做什麼啊？我要打掃房間。房間亂七八糟的。
B: I have no idea. I might sleep late in the morning. But I am considering whether I should go to see my mom or not.	我還不知道呢。我可能早上睡個懶覺。但是我在考慮要不要去看看我媽媽。
A: Then I'll take exercise and take a shower. Exercise helps me keep healthy.	之後我會去運動，然後洗個澡。運動有助於身體健康。
B: Really? Does it work?	真的嗎？有效嗎？
A: Certainly! You can have a try, too!	當然！你也可以試試看啊！

 關鍵單字要認得

clean ... room *ph.* 打掃房間	**My mom asked me to clean my room .** → 我媽要我打掃房間。
mess *n.* 亂七八糟、凌亂	**Your room is totally a mess** → 你的房間完全是一團亂。
I have no idea *ph.* 不知道	**I have no idea what we should do next .** → 我不知道我們接下來該做什麼。

129

consider	**I am considering going shopping on weekends.**
v. 考慮	→ 我在考慮週末去購物。

exercise	**I hate to do exercises.**
n. 運動	→ 我痛恨運動。

healthy	**Eating different kinds of fruit every day is healthy.**
adj. 健康的	→ 每天吃不同水果很健康。

 一定要會的萬用句

❶ I have to clean my room. It's a mess.

→ 我要打掃房間。房間亂七八糟的。

❷ I might sleep late in the morning.

→ 我可能早上睡個懶覺。

❸ Exercise helps me keep healthy.

→ 運動有助於身體健康。

❹ You can have a try, too!

→ 你也可以試試看啊！

 我們也能這樣說

❶ Tomorrow we will begin to work.

→ 明天就要開始上班了。

❷ What is your plan when you come back from holiday?

→ 渡假回來後，你有什麼計畫嗎？

❸ I have to take a shower.

→ 我必須洗個澡。

❹ How time flies! → 時間過得真快。

常見錯誤不要犯

句子中是否要加不定式是學習英文的重點之一，要避免 "Exercise helps me to keep healthy?" 的錯誤説法。

正確説法是 "Exercise helps me keep healthy."

正確的表達是 help sb. do sth.，沒有後面加不定式的用法！有類似用法的單字還有：let sb. do sth. / make sb. do sth. 等。

常見句型一起學

★ 是否要……？

Whether   I should go to see my mom   or   not.

Whether   +   子句   + or   not

Whether...or not? 這種省略句型的意思是「是否要……？」。

以下是其他的相關例句：

▶ **I was wondering whether to go upstairs or not.**
→ 我不知是否該上樓。

▶ **She was wondering whether to go home or not.**
→ 她猶豫不定，是回家還是不回呢。

▶ **I don't know whether to go or not.**
→ 我不知道該去還是不去。

▶ **Whether they do it or not matters little.**
→ 他們做不做這件事都沒什麼關係。

▶ **I do not care whether it rains or not.**
→ 我不在乎會不會下雨。

Part 2
公事公辦

01 自我介紹

 情境對話 🎧 Track 41

隨著網際網路越來越發達,遠距離上班甚至是跨國上班都不再是不可能的事,而「在家上班」也是新興的工作型態,因此視訊會議就變得非常重要,學會視訊會議可以用的英文對未來會很有幫助。

A: Hello, everyone. I'm your new colleague Cathy. Nice to meet you.	大家好,我是你們的新同事凱西,很高興見到你們。
B: Nice to meet you, too. So tell us more about yourself.	我們也很高興見到妳。告訴我們更多關於妳的事情吧!
A: I am trying to make my dream come true. I hope I can make progress with all of you.	我在努力實現自己的夢想。我希望我能在這裡與各位一起進步。
B: Then do you have any expectations from us?	那麼,妳對我們有什麼期望呢?
A: I hope you can give me a hand if I have difficulties in my work someday.	我希望之後要是在工作上遇到了困難,你們能夠伸出援手。
B: No problem! We'd love to help you if you need.	沒問題!如果妳需要的話,我們很願意幫妳。

 關鍵單字要認得

colleague
n. 同事

Let's throw a party for our new colleague.
→ 來為我們的新同事辦個派對吧。

134

make progress *ph.* 取得進展、進步	**The project is making great progress.** → 計畫取得絕佳的進展。
expectation *n.* 期望	**She has high expectations for her son.** → 她對她兒子有很高的期望。
give... a hand *ph.* 幫某人的忙	**Could you give me a hand?** → 你可以幫我一個忙嗎？

- -

 一定要會的萬用句

❶ I'm your new colleague. → 我是你們的新同事。

❷ Tell us more about yourself.

　　→ 告訴我們更多關於你的事情吧！

❸ I hope I can make progress with all of you.

　　→ 我希望我能與各位一起進步。

❹ Do you have any expectations from us?

　　→ 你對我們有什麼期望呢？

 我們也能這樣說

❶ I hope I can assist you in work.

　　→ 我希望我能在工作上協助你。

❷ I am new here. → 我是這裡的新人。

❸ We can help each other. → 我們可以互相幫助。

❹ I will introduce myself briefly.

　　→ 我來做個簡單的自我介紹。

❺ What do you want to get in the company?

　　→ 你想在這家公司得到什麼？

在英文文法中,使役動詞後的動詞該如何變化是個重點,要注意別説出 "I am trying to make my dream coming true." 的錯誤句子。

正確的説法是 "I am trying to make my dream come true."

片語 come true 意為「實現、成為事實、成真」。由於 make 後面用動詞原形,所以在此不能用 coming true 而應該用 come true。

常見句型一起學

★ 某人希望……

I hope   you can give me a hand   if I have difficulty in my work someday.

I hope +   that 子句   +   其他

此句型表達「某人希望……」,you can give me a hand是省略了 that 的子句,它是動詞 hope 的受詞。以下是其他的相關例句:

▶ **I hope that I can find that girl.**
→ 我希望能找到那個女孩。

▶ **I hope that I didn't misunderstand you.**
→ 我希望我沒有誤解你。

▶ **I hope that I have mentioned all the points.**
→ 我希望我提到了所有的要點。

▶ **I hope that you will have a wonderful journey.**
→ 我希望你會有個精彩的旅程。

▶ **I hope that you can come earlier.**
→ 我希望你能早點來。

02 從基層做起

 情境對話　∩ Track 42

有一份工作是很重要的，而一份新的工作多半要從基層做起，新進職員進到公司就要先了解公司的大小事。

A: Nice to meet you, Sara. I am In charge of this department. You can call me Tom.	很高興見到妳，莎拉。我是這個部門的負責人，妳可以叫我湯姆。
B: I am eager to know about my job.	我希望可以儘快知道工作內容。
A: In our company, we expect our new staff to work from the bottom and work up later on.	在我們這個公司，希望新員工能從基層做起，再逐漸往上升職。
B: I get It. I will do my best.	我明白。我會好好努力的。
A: That's good. I believe you can make it.	很好。我相信妳能做到這一點。
B: Thank you. So I'll begin to work now.	謝謝您。那麼我現在開始工作了。

 關鍵單字要認得

meet 🔳 會見	**I'll meet the client tomorrow.** → 我明天會去見委託人。
in charge of 🔳 負責	**Mary is in charge of this project.** → 瑪麗負責這個計畫。

eager to	**David is eager to buy his own house.**
ph. 渴望	→ 大衛渴望買自己的房子。

begin	**The meeting begins at ten.**
v. 開始	→ 會議十點開始。

• •

 一定要會的萬用句

1 I am in charge of this department.

→ 我是這個部門的負責人。

2 I am eager to know about my job.

→ 我希望可以儘快知道工作內容。

3 I will do my best. → 我會好好努力的。

4 I believe you can make it. → 我相信你能做到。

 我們也能這樣說

1 This is our manager, Rick.

→ 這是我們的經理，瑞克。

2 Can you tell me something about my job?

→ 能跟我談談我的工作內容嗎？

3 I really appreciate this chance.

→ 真的很感謝有這個機會。

4 He is in charge of this department.

→ 他負責這個部門。

5 I will do my best in the work.

→ 我會竭盡全力工作的。

常見錯誤不要犯

在英文文法中,動詞的存在非常重要,要注意別說出 "I eager to know about my job." 的錯誤句子。

正確的說法是 "I am eager to know about my job."

eager 為形容詞,意為「熱切的、渴望的」。片語 be eager to 意為「渴望要做、熱切想做」。在此,第一句缺少謂語動詞,必須要有 be 動詞才行。

常見句型一起學

★ sb. believe+that 引導的子句

I believe you can make it.
主詞 + believe + (that) 子句

這個句型用 that 引導的子句來表示 believe 的內容。我們也可以把 believe 換成是 think / guess 等動詞。

以下是其他的相關例句:

▶ **Do you believe he did this?**
→ 你相信是他做的嗎?

▶ **I can't believe that he attended this meeting at last!**
→ 我真不敢相信,他最後還是來參加這次會議了。

03 現在要做什麼工作

 情境對話　∩ Track 43

和同事間的溝通一向是工作中重要的一環，不管是自己原先的業務範圍或後來被交辦的工作，都會需要和同事合作，絕對要掌握好同事間的溝通技巧！

A: Have you finished the talk with David? Are you available now?	妳和大衛已經談完了？妳現在有空嗎？
B: Yeah, we have finished talking. And what am I expected to do now?	是的，我們已經談完了。那我現在要做些什麼工作呢？
A: As a new employee, you are going to be responsible for some basic tasks first.	身為一個新員工，妳必須要先負責一些基本的工作。
B: I see. If I have some problems, may I speak out directly?	我明白了。如果我遇到問題的話，我能直接説出來嗎？
A: Don't hesitate to tell us if you have a problem.	有問題就直接發問！
B: OK! And thanks for your instruction.	好的。謝謝您的指導！

 關鍵單字要認得

available *adj.* 有空	**I'm not available to go the party next Sunday.** → 我沒辦法參加下個星期天的派對。
be responsible for *ph.* 對……負責	**He is responsible for the project.** → 他要負責這個計劃。

| **speak out**
ph. 說出 | **If you have any problem, please speak out.**
→ 如果你有任何問題，請說出來。 |

| **instruction**
n. 指導 | **Please give me clear instructions on what to do next.**
→ 關於接下來要怎麼做，請給我明確的指示。 |

• •

 一定要會的萬用句

① Are you available now? → 你現在有空嗎？

② We have finished talking. → 我們已經談完了。

③ If I have some problems, may I speak out directly?

→ 如果我遇到問題的話，我能直接說出來嗎？

④ Don't hesitate to tell us if you have a problem.

→ 有問題就直接發問！

 我們也能這樣說

① It must be a challenging job.

→ 這一定是個有挑戰性的工作。

② I am available now. → 我現在有空。

③ The harder you work, the more progress you make.

→ 你越努力，就越進步。

④ You should be responsible for his injury.

→ 你應該對他的傷負責。

⑤ It's my pleasure to work with you.

→ 很高興跟你們一起工作。

⑥ May I have the honor to know your name?

→ 我能知道你的名字嗎？

即使意思相近，不同的單字也未必能通用，如 "I look." 就是一個錯誤的句子，"I see." 才是正確的。

雖然 look 和 see 都有「看見」的意思，但是 I see 是「我知道」的意思，相當於 I know。所以不能用 I look。

 常見句型一起學

★ 現在完成式

Have you　finished　the talk　with David?

Have you　+　過去分詞　+　受詞　+　其他

典型的現在完成式，句型即為「have＋過去分詞」。

以下是其他的相關例句：

▶ **Have you completed it?**
→ 你完成了嗎？

▶ **I have stayed in the city for 4 years.**
→ 我已經在這座城市待四年了。

▶ **Have you heard of that?**
→ 你聽說了嗎？

▶ **I have bought it.**
→ 我已經買下它了。

▶ **Have you read that story?**
→ 你讀過那個故事嗎？

 情境對話 ∩ **Track 44**

一份工作的好與壞，最重要的不是薪資，但不可否認的是薪資也是相當重要的一環，要怎麼與雇主討論工作待遇也是一定要學會的！

A: Mike, how about my salary? Would you meet all my requirements?	邁克，那我的薪水呢？你會答應我所提出的要求嗎？
B: Congrats, Sarah. We decided to agree to all of them. Our company provides every employee here with a good welfare so that they can concentrate on their work.	恭喜妳，莎拉。我們決定同意全部條件。我們公司給每一位員工提供相當好的待遇，就是要讓他們能專心工作。
A: Wow, thank you. And also, can you tell me something else, like attendance record?	哇，真的太感謝了！另外，請告訴我一些該注意的事情吧？比如出缺勤之類的。
B: You need to work eight hours per day, from nine a.m. to six p.m. Every month you get three days off except the weekend and some important holidays.	妳需要每天工作八小時，早上九點上班，下午六點下班。除了重大節日和週末外，每個月還有三天假。
A: Wow, it sounds not bad.	哇，聽起來還不錯。

 關鍵單字要認得

salary
n 薪資

John asked for a ten percent salary increase.
→ 約翰要求10%的加薪。

meet ... requirements *ph.* 滿足要求	**We need to meet all customers' requirements.** → 我們要滿足客戶所有的要求。
concentrate on *ph.* 專心於……	**David needs to concentrate on his work.** → 大衛需要在工作上專心。
attendance record *ph.* 出勤記錄	**Please check your attendance record.** → 請確認你的出勤紀錄。
weekend *n.* 週末	**We plan to watch movies this weekend.** → 我們計畫這個週末看電影。

• •

 一定要會的萬用句

❶ Would you meet all my requirements? → 你會滿足我所有的要求嗎?

❷ We decided to agree to all of them. → 我們決定全部同意。

❸ Can you tell me something else? → 請告訴我一些別的事情吧?

❹ It sounds not bad. → 聽起來還不錯。

 我們也能這樣說

❶ What about my wage? → 我的薪水如何呢?

❷ Is there anything you want to tell me?

→ 還有別的事情要告訴我嗎?

❸ Does your company give out annual bonuses to its employees?

→ 你公司會發年終獎金給員工嗎?

❹ Don't come in late and leave early. → 不要遲到早退。

❺ I hope I can find a job with an excellent boss and a high salary.

→ 我希望找到一個老闆好、薪水高的工作。

 常見錯誤不要犯

即使意思相近，不同的單字也未必能通用，如 "Will we talk about the welfare policies?" 就是一個錯誤的句子，"Shall we talk about the welfare policies?" 才是正確的。

will 和 shall 在問句上的區別是：shall 一般用於第一人稱，比如 shall we go to the park? 而 will 一般用於第二、三人稱 will you go with me? 但如果是直述句，will就沒有限制了。

👍 **常見句型一起學**

★ 某人需要做某事

You   need   to work   eight hours per day.
　主詞　　+　need　+　不定詞　　+　　　　介詞片語

sb. need to do sth. 這個句型表達的意思是某人需要做某事。need 後面接續的是不定詞，而在不定詞後面可以接續介詞片語，也可以接續該動詞的受詞。

以下是其他的相關例句：

▶ **We need to work hard.**
→ 我們需要繼續努力。

▶ **We need to give him authority to do that.**
→ 我們需要給他辦此事的權力。

05 申請公司電子信箱

 情境對話　∩ Track 45

在處理公事的時候，多半有專用的電子信箱以便員工和合作單位聯絡，員工間互相聯絡也可能會使用公司專用的電子信箱，電子信箱在工作上是不可或缺的。

A: I need a company email address before I start working. But I don't know how to apply for it.	我開始工作之前先要申請一個公司電子信箱，但是我不知道該怎麼申請。
B: Right, we must have an email in order to contact each other immediately. And with an enterprise email, we can enjoy a high safety service as well as a high speed service.	對，我們都必須要有一個電子信箱以便即時聯繫彼此。有了公司電子信箱後，我們就可以享受高安全性與高速度的服務了。
A: And what's the procedure for having one?	要申請的話，有什麼步驟嗎？
B: First, you must enter the management system of our company. Then you can start your application.	首先你必須進入我們公司的管理系統，然後才能申請。
A: Do I need a company code?	我需要一個公司密碼嗎？
B: That's right. I'll give it to you later on.	沒錯。我稍後給你。

 關鍵單字要認得

apply for *ph.* 申請	**She sent a cover letter and applied for a new job.** → 她寄了一封求職信並申請一份新工作。

in order to *ph.* 為了……	**May spent a lot of time studying in order to pass the exam.** → 梅為了通過考試而花了很多時間讀書。
procedure *n.* 程序、步驟	**We have to establish procedures for dealing with customers.** → 我們要建立和客戶溝通的程序。
code *n.* 密碼、代號	**Their letters were written in code.** → 他們的信件是用密碼寫的。

• •

 一定要會的萬用句

❶ I need a company email address before I start working.

→ 我開始工作之前先要申請一個公司電子信箱。

❷ I don't know how to apply for it. → 我不知道該怎麼申請。

❸ What's the procedure for getting one?

→ 要申請的話,有什麼步驟嗎?

❹ I'll give it to you later on. → 我稍後給你。

 我們也能這樣說

❶ It's so difficult for me to finish this task.

→ 完成這項工作對我來說很難。

❷ Do you see my attachment in the email?

→ 你有看見我郵件裡的附件嗎?

❸ I need enough data to fill in this form.

→ 我需要足夠的資料來填寫這個表格。

❹ It took me one week to get through all my work.

→ 我花了一星期才做完所有的工作。

❺ This plan sounds reasonable. → 這個計畫聽起來不錯!

that子句和不定詞的用法大不相同，如 "We must have an email in order that contact each other immediately." 就是一個錯誤的句子。

正確的説法是 "We must have an email in order to contact each other immediately."

片語 in order that 和 in order to 都是「為了」的意思。但是 in order that 後面要接完整的句子，而 in order to 後面只能加動詞原形。

👍 常見句型一起學

★ 既……又……

We   can enjoy   a high safety service   as well as   a high speed service.
主詞 + 動詞 +   名詞   + as well as +   名詞

sb.＋動詞＋名詞＋as well as＋名詞，這個句型中表示的是前後名詞的內容同時擁有或是存在。其中，as well as 的意思就是「……和……；既……又……」。在 as well as 前後的內容的成分必須相同，二者是並列的，可以是名詞，也可以是形容詞或動詞片語。

以下是其他的相關例句：

▶ **He went to the party as well as his brother.**
→ 他和他哥哥都出席了晚會。

▷ **He was kind as well as sensible.**
→ 他既懂道理又善良。

▶ **You can bring your child as well as your husband here.**
→ 你可以把你的丈夫和孩子都帶來。

▷ **You can take this dress as well as this coat.**
→ 你可以拿走這件裙子和這件外套。

▶ **He grows rice as well as vegetables.**
→ 他既種稻也種菜。

情境對話 🎧 **Track 46**

沒有十全十美的產品，若產品不盡人意，讓客戶想要退款的話，可以跟客服反映。
而在工作上也可能會遇到希望退款的客戶，要如何和客戶溝通以達成雙贏的效果，
也是一門學問。

A: Hello, this is ABC Company. What can I do for you?	您好，這裡是 ABC 公司。有什麼能為您效勞？
B: There are serious problems in your products. I want a full refund for my loss.	你們的產品存在嚴重的問題。我要求你們對我的損失進行全額退款。
A: Sorry sir. We will deal with it. We are a company with high reputation in this trade, so you can trust us absolutely!	抱歉，先生，我們會進行處理。我們在這一行業中信譽良好，所以您完全可以相信我們。
B: Good. I hope you can reply to me ASAP.	很好。我希望你們儘快答覆我。
A: No problem. And may I pass you to our colleague responsible for after-sale services? He is the person in charge.	好的，沒問題。請允許我把您的電話轉到負責售後服務的同事那去好嗎？
B: Okay.	好的。

關鍵單字要認得

**refund for ...
loss**

ph. 全額退款

The smartphone she bought is broken, so she asked for a refund for her loss.

→ 她買的智慧型手機壞掉了，所以她要求全額退款。

reputation *n.* 名譽	**The company established a great reputation.** → 公司建立了很好的信譽。
trade *n.* 行業；交易	**He made up his mind to work in the book trade.** → 他下定決心要在書籍相關行業工作。
reply *v.* 回覆	**Please reply the message as soon as possible.** → 請儘快回覆訊息。

一定要會的萬用句

❶ There are serious problems in your products.

→ 你們的產品存在嚴重的問題。

❷ I want a full refund for my loss.

→ 我要求對我的損失進行全額退款。

❸ We will deal with it. → 我們會進行處理。

❹ I hope you can reply to me ASAP! → 我希望你們儘快答覆我。

我們也能這樣說

❶ I'm calling on behalf of Mr. Tom.

→ 我代表湯姆先生打電話給你。

❷ What time would suit you best?

→ 什麼時候您比較方便呢？

❸ May I take a message? → 你需要留言嗎？

❹ Do you know when he'll be back?

→ 你知道他何時回來嗎？

❺ I'm sorry, he's not in the office now.

→ 很抱歉，他現在不在辦公室。

常見錯誤不要犯

在英文中，介係詞是一個句子中很重要的存在，若是忽略介係詞就可能說出 "I hope you can reply for me ASAP!" 這樣錯誤的句子。

正確的説法是 "I hope you can reply to me ASAP!"

片語 reply to sb. 意為「答覆某人」， 其中的介係詞應為 to，具有指向性。 不能用 reply for sb.。另外，要注意的是 ASAP 是 as soon as possible 的縮寫。

👍 **常見句型一起學**

★ 我可以……嗎？

May I　pass　you　　to　　our colleague?

May I ＋ 動詞 ＋ 受詞 ＋ 介係詞 ＋ 受詞

這個句型的意思是「我可以……嗎？」，是一種用於委婉提出自己建議的句型。可以顯示出説話人的禮貌和對聽話者的尊重。以下是其他的相關例句：

▶ **May I come in?**
→ 我能進來嗎？

▷ **May I eat this apple?**
→ 我能吃這個蘋果嗎？

▶ **May I go with you?**
→ 我能和你一起去嗎？

▷ **May I have a look at it?**
→ 我能看一下嗎？

▶ **May I dance with you?**
→ 能和你跳一曲嗎？

情境對話　∩ **Track 47**

因為公事要聯絡不同部門或其他公司的人時，可能會遇到聯絡不到對方的情況，這種時候就要留下訊息，請他人幫忙轉達。

A: Hello, Blue Sky Corporation. Jane speaking.	你好，這裡是藍天公司。我是珍。
B: Excuse me, may I speak to Ben? I couldn't reach him. It's urgent!	打擾了，我想要找班。我聯絡不到他。我有急事！
A: Please hold on for a moment… I am sorry, but Ben is out. Would you like to leave a message?	請稍等一下。很抱歉，班不在公司。你要留言嗎？
B: Please tell Ben that our goods have reached the customs. We need a truck to transport the goods. And also when he dispatches the truck, please ask him to let the driver bring the receipt.	請告訴班，我們的貨物已經到達海關了。我們需要一輛車來運送。還請告訴他派車來的時候，請讓司機把收據也一起帶過來。
A: Ok, I have written them down. You mean our goods are inspected in customs? I will tell him as soon as possible.	好的，我把它們都記下來了。你是說我們的貨物在海關受檢嗎？我會儘快告訴他的。

關鍵單字要認得

for a moment　　　**I didn't know what to say for a moment.**
ph. 一會兒　　　　　→ 我一時之間不知道該說什麼。

152

dispatch
☑ 派遣、發送

David dispatched a truck to the factory.
→ 大衛派遣一輛卡車去工廠。

goods
☑ 貨物;商品

The goods in this store are on sale.
→ 這間店的商品正在特價。

inspect
☑ 詳細檢查

We need to inspect the goods right now.
→ 我們要馬上檢查商品。

 一定要會的萬用句

① Please hold on for a moment. → 請稍等一下。

② Would you like to leave a message? → 你要留言嗎?

③ We need a truck to transport the goods.
　　→ 我們需要一輛車來運送貨物。

④ I have written them down. → 我把它們都記下來了。

 我們也能這樣說

① Hello, is that Mr. Chen's office?
　　→ 喂,請問是陳先生的辦公室嗎?

② Hello, this is Catharine speaking.
　　→ 喂,我是凱薩琳。

③ Please connect me to room 403.
　　→ 請幫我接 403 號房。

④ Could I leave a message?
　　→ 我可以留話嗎?

⑤ Please tell Jenny that she must call me back in one hour.
　　→ 請告訴珍妮務必要在一個小時之內回電給我。

在英語文化中，通話與實際見面的招呼語不大相同，如 "I'm Jane." 是不會使用的句子。

正確的說法是 "Jane speaking."

因為在通話中，只聞其聲不見其人，所以報出身分的方式是說誰在講話。若兩人有見面的話，就可以使用 "I'm Jane." 了。

常見句型一起學

★ 表現禮貌的祈使句

Please ask him to let the driver bring the receipt.

Please + 動詞原形 + 受詞 + 不定詞 + 其他

此祈使句是表現禮貌的用法，很客氣或委婉的請求。please 放在句尾時，要用逗號和前面的部分隔開。有時候也會是加強要求的語氣。

以下是其他的相關例句：

▶ **Please make yourself at home.**
→ 請把這裡當成自己家！（多用於主人請客人不要拘束）

▶ **Let me have a look at it, please.**
→ 請讓我看看。

08 聯絡客戶

從事業務相關工作時，要適時聯絡客戶，不只是瞭解產品的使用情形，更是與客戶培養交情，讓未來的合作更加順利。

A: Hello, Mike, I am Megan from BIO Corp. Are our products still in good condition now? You know, all of them have first class quality. Besides, we use advanced technology.	您好，邁克，我是 BIO 公司的梅根。我們的產品現在是否使用狀況良好呢？你知道的，它們的品質可都是一流的。此外，我們還採用了先進技術。
B: Yeah! Your company is developing so fast, so is ours. Maybe I will plan to buy more in the near future.	很好！你們公司發展真快啊，我們也是。也許不久的將來我們還要計畫買更多呢！
A: Absolutely! Do you mind my visiting there at your convenience?	當然！您介意我在您方便的時候拜訪您嗎？
B: Of course not. Anytime!	當然不介意。什麼時候都行！

關鍵單字要認得

in good condition *ph.* 狀況良好	**All of our products are in good condition.** → 我們所有的產品都狀況良好。
first class *ph.* 一流的	**David did a first-class job of painting the walls .** → 大衛粉刷牆壁做得非常好。

155

quality _n._ 品質	**We value the quality of our goods.** → 我們重視我們的商品品質。
use _v._ 採用	**We use white paint to cover the doodle on the wall.** → 我們用白色油漆來附蓋掉牆上的塗鴉。
convenience _n._ 方便	**I want the convenience of living close to office.** → 我想要有住得離辦公室近的便利性。

• •

 一定要會的萬用句

❶ Are our products still in good condition now?

→ 我們的產品現在是否使用狀況良好呢？

❷ We use advanced technology. → 我們採用了先進技術。

❸ Do you mind my visiting there at your convenience?

→ 您介意我在您方便的時候拜訪您嗎？

❹ Anytime! → 什麼時候都行！

 我們也能這樣說

❶ This is our latest product. → 這是我們的最新產品。

❷ Our product is much better than before, but we're selling it at nearly the same price.

→ 我們的產品比以前好很多，但是我們幾乎以同樣的價格銷售。

❸ I am sure we can offer the best products and services to you.

→ 我保證我們能為您提供最好的產品和服務。

❹ You are one of our oldest clients. → 您是我們的老客戶了。

❺ We appreciate your business for the past three years.

→ 我們非常重視這三年來與您的合作。

常見錯誤不要犯

在英語文法中，片語有其固定的介系詞用法，如 "Are our products still at good condition now?" 是不會使用的句子。

正確的說法是 "Are our products still in good condition now?"

片語 in good condition 是「情況良好、身體健康」的意思，它是固定搭配，其中的介係詞為 in 而不是 at。in ... condition 意為處於一種……的狀況。

👍 常見句型一起學

★ 表示前後兩者狀況相同的倒裝句

Your company is developing so fast, so is ours.

主句 +　　　　　　　　　　　　so + be動詞 + 主詞（倒裝）

so＋be 動詞＋主詞，這是一個比較典型的倒裝句型。其中 so 引導的句子與前面主句引導的句子情形類似，或是前後兩者狀況相同。其中的 be 動詞還可以根據主詞的動詞，用助動詞 do / does 來替代。但是需要注意助動詞單複數的變化。

以下是其他的相關例句：

▶ **He is a student, so am I.**
→ 我和他都是學生。

▶ **This man is a teacher, so are they.**
→ 這個人和他們都是老師。

▶ **I think in this way, so does my manager.**
→ 我和我們經理的想法不謀而合。

▶ **She loves dog, so does her brother.**
→ 她和她哥哥都喜歡狗。

▶ **The boy likes studying, so do these children.**
→ 這個男孩和那些孩子都一樣很喜歡讀書。

09 您會對我們的產品感興趣的

 **情境對話** ∩ Track 49

鞏固舊客戶之餘，也要積極開發潛在的顧客群。主動出擊，向他人介紹公司提供的服務及產品，努力提升產品銷售業績吧！

A: Hello, Can I speak to Mr. Tom?	您好，請接湯姆先生。
B: Speaking.	我就是。
A: This is Sarah from Blue Sky Corp. I am sure you will be interested in our products.	我是藍天公司的莎拉。我相信您會對我們的產品很感興趣的。
B: What does your company provide?	你們公司提供什麼產品呢？
A: Our company offers customers all kinds of electronic products. You can get them at a lower price.	我們公司生產各種電子產品，而且提供您較低的價格。
B: Sounds good! I will consider a future cooperation between us.	聽起來不錯。我會考慮一下雙方未來的合作。
A: Could I have your email so that I can send you some information of our products?	那麼您可以給我您的電子信箱嗎？以便我給您發些我們的產品資料。
B: OK.	好的。

 關鍵單字要認得

speak	**This is Amy speaking.**
☑ 說話	→ 我是艾米，請說。

provide ☑ 提供	**We provide legal service in Taiwan.** → 我們提供在台灣的法律服務。
offer ☑ 提供	**The restaurant offers free meals for the refugees.** → 餐廳提供免費餐點給難民。
all kinds of *ph.* 各種	**Jimmy's Bakery sales all kinds of pastry.** → 吉米烘焙坊有賣各種糕點。
sounds good *ph.* 聽起來不錯	**Sarah's summer plan sounds good.** → 莎拉的暑期計畫聽起來不錯。

・ ・

 一定要會的萬用句

❶ I am sure you will be interested in our products.

→ 我相信您會對我們的產品很感興趣的。

❷ What does your company provide? → 你們公司提供什麼產品呢？

❸ You can get them at a lower price. → 我們會提供您較低的價格。

❹ I will consider a future cooperation between us.

→ 我會考慮一下雙方未來的合作。

 我們也能這樣說

❶ Do you think our price is reasonable? → 你認為我們的價格合理嗎？

❷ We would be very happy to send samples to you.

→ 我會很樂意為你提供樣品。

❸ Our company provides customers with a lot of products.

→ 我們提供的產品眾多。

❹ Do you have our latest products? → 您購買了我們的最新產品了嗎？

❺ What about its performance? → 性能怎麼樣呢？

在英語文法中，比較級有其固定的用法，如 "You can get them at a more low price." 是不會使用的句子。

正確的說法是 "You can get them at a lower price."

一般單音節詞和少數以 -er，-ow 結尾的雙音節詞，比較級在後面加 -er，最高級在後面加 -est。形容詞 low 的比較級形式直接加 er，即 lower。其他雙音節詞和多音節詞，比較級在前面加more，最高級在前面加 most。

常見句型一起學

★ 表示對某事感興趣的句型

You　will be interested in　　our products.

主詞　+　　　　be interested in　　　　+　　　事物

sb. be interested in sth. 某人對某事感興趣。這個句型主要用在某人對某件事情感興趣，或者想知道某件事情的情況下。我們還可以用另外一種表達方式：sb. has/have interest to sth.

以下是其他的相關例句：

▶ **What is it in particular you are interested in?**
→ 你對哪些產品感興趣？

▶ **He is quite interested in living in the countryside.**
→ 他對住在鄉下很感興趣。

▶ **In fact, I am not interested in this exhibition.**
→ 事實上，我對這次的展覽並不感興趣。

▶ **We are very interested in what he said.**
→ 我們對他所說的很感興趣。

▶ **Are you interested in this?**
→ 你對這個感興趣嗎？

10 討論工作

 **情境對話** ∩ **Track 50**

業績表現不盡理想嗎？沒關係，開會期間，大家一起集思廣益，找到問題的癥結點，擬定出相應的策略吧！

A: Hello, everyone. Today I want to talk about our work.	大家好，今天我想討論一下我們的工作。
B: Fine. What's going on?	好的。發生什麼狀況？
A: Our business is in a mess. The sales are very down in American market recently. I think we can do better than that. I hope you can give me some good suggestions.	我們的生意現在很糟糕。最近在美國市場上的銷售額很低。我們應該可以做得比這更好的。希望大家能給一些好的意見。
B: I think our propaganda isn't enough. When customers see our products, they don't regard it as a well-known brand. So we can do something in this aspect.	我認為是我們的宣傳不夠。消費者看到我們的產品，都不認為它們是名牌產品。因此，我們可以在這個領域改進一下。
A: Good point! Any other opinions?	說得很好！還有其他什麼建議嗎？
B: And the attitude towards customers should be more polite and gentler.	還有就是對待客戶的態度要更加禮貌溫和。

 關鍵單字要認得

talk about
ph. 談論

We talk about our future a lot.
→ 我們經常談論起我們的未來規畫。

in a mess *ph.* 糟糕	**The postal service was in a mess during the holiday season.** → 假期期間的郵寄服務很糟糕。
market *n.* 市場	**Our company is planning to expand the target market.** → 本公司計畫將拓展目標客群市場。
suggestion *n.* 建議	**Any suggestion for the upcoming exhibition?** → 大家對於即將到來的展覽有任何建議嗎？
well-known brand *ph.* 名牌	**Coca-Cola is considered a well-known brand around the world.** → 可口可樂被認為是一個世界知名的品牌。
opinion *n.* 意見、建議	**In my opinion, the red hat is better than the blue one.** → 在我看來，那頂紅色的帽子比藍色的好看。

- -

 一定要會的萬用句

❶ I want to talk about our work. → 我想討論一下我們的工作。

❷ What's going on? → 發生什麼狀況？

❸ Our business is in a mess. → 我們的生意現在很糟糕。

❹ We can do something in this aspect. → 我們可以在這個領域改進一下。

 我們也能這樣說

❶ Do you have any opinion about this matter? → 你對這件事情有何意見？

❷ We still need a new plan to improve our work.
→ 我們需要有個全新的計畫來改進現有的工作。

❸ I think you didn't take this point into consideration.
→ 我認為你沒考慮到這一點。

❹ We can cooperate with other companies. → 我們可以和其他企業聯手。

❺ A publicity campaign might be a good choice.
→ 媒體宣傳是個不錯的選擇。

在英語文法中,片語有其固定的用法,如 "Our business is at a mess." 是不會使用的句子。

正確的説法是 "Our business is in a mess."

片語 in a mess 意為「一團糟、亂糟糟、一片混亂、亂七八糟」。是固定搭配的片語,其中的介係詞是 in 而不是at。

 常見句型一起學

★ 表示「可以做得更好」的句型

We can do better than that.

主詞 + 助動詞 + 動詞 + 副詞比較級 + than + 名詞

主詞加(動詞+副詞比較級+than),再加上名詞,這是一個典型的比較句型。意思是「……可以更……」。主要用於前後兩者情況懸殊,或是有差距的情形之下。

以下是其他的相關例句:

▶ **I know he is better than the rest.**
→ 我知道他比其他人都優秀。

▷ **You look better than before.**
→ 你的氣色比以前好多了。

▶ **My son did better than last time yesterday.**
→ 我兒子昨天比上次做的出色多了。

▷ **He can do better than this anytime.**
→ 他一定能比這次做得更好。

▶ **If you can't do better than John, you'll be fired.**
→ 如果你做得不如約翰好,那麼你就要被解雇。

11 避免糟糕的結果

 情境對話　∩ Track 51

市場變化瞬息萬變，意外變故總是打得大家措手不及。對於能夠預見的局面，我們能夠積極準備；對無法預期的事件，我們也可以努力克服！

A: Mike, what do you think of this issue?	麥克，對這個問題你有什麼看法？
B: There are many factors leading to this result. If we had known it in advance, we would have avoided this.	有很多因素促成了這結果。要是我們事前知道就好了，就可以避免這樣的結果。
A: Yes, but the fact is that no one can predict that.	是啊，但是事實上，沒有人可以預料到。
B: I think the most important thing is how to change such a terrible situation soon.	我認為現在最重要的事情就是採取措施，迅速改變當前糟糕的局面。
A: I agree. Only by multiplying our efforts can we get out of difficulties.	我同意。只有再加倍努力，我們才能擺脫困境。
B: Yes, it is!	沒錯！

 關鍵單字要認得

factor *n.* 因素	**The global pandemic is one of the main factors that cause the bankruptcy of the restaurant.** → 全球疫情是導致這家餐廳破產的因素之一。
lead to *ph.* 導致	**Peter's lack of practice leads to his failure at the audition.** → 彼得的缺乏練習最終導致他樂團面試失敗。

164

in advance *ph.* 提前	**I'll inform you in advance.** → 我會提前通知你。
predict *v.* 預料	**It is hard to predict one's future.** → 個人的未來是難以預料的。
get out of *ph.* 擺脫	**I'm eager to get out of this situation.** → 我急於擺脫眼前的狀況。

 一定要會的萬用句

➊ What do you think of this issue?

　→ 對這個問題你有什麼看法？

➋ If we had known it in advance, we would have avoided this.

　→ 要是我們事前知道就好了，就可以避免這樣的結果。

➌ Only by multiplying our efforts can we get out of difficulties.

　→ 只有再加倍努力，我們才能擺脫困境。

 我們也能這樣說

➊ You can take a break for fifteen minutes.

　→ 你們可以休息十五分鐘。

➋ We have to continue discussing.　→ 我們需要繼續討論。

➌ The meeting was delayed because of several people's absence.

　→ 由於幾個人缺席了，所以會議延遲。

➍ We must put this thing at the first place.

　→ 我們必須把這件事放在首位。

➎ There are some ways to solve it.

　→ 有幾個辦法可以解決這件事情。

在英語文法中，千萬要注意介系詞的用法，如 "What do you think this issue?" 是不會使用的句子。

正確的說法是 "What do you think of this issue?"

詢問什麼東西怎麼樣可以用這個句型：What do you think of sth.? 如果後面有名詞，那麼就一定要有介係詞of。但是如果後面沒有名詞，單獨說：What do you think? 也是可以的。

常見句型一起學

★ 詢問「如何⋯⋯」的省略句型

How to change   such a situation?

How to　+　動詞原形　+　　　名詞

how to...? 這是一個省略句型。其中省略了主詞。以上面的句子來說，完整的說法應該是How can we change such a situation? 省略的時候，how 後面接續的是 to 加上動詞原形，再加受詞。

以下是其他的相關例句：

▶ **Will you tell me how to use it?**
→ 請告訴我怎樣使用這個？

▶ **Does your husband know how to cook?**
→ 你丈夫會做飯嗎？

▶ **Do you know how to love?**
→ 你知道如何去愛嗎？

▶ **Have you considered how to get there?**
→ 你是否考慮過如何到那裡去？

▶ **Could you tell me how to copy that?**
→ 你能告訴我如何複製那個嗎？

12 進行產品宣傳工作

 情境對話　∩ **Track 52**

好的產品宣傳策略能帶來大量商機，而了解目標客群則是制定宣傳策略的第一步。
馬上來看看如何討論產品宣傳工作吧！

A: According to our general manager's speech, our department is planning to advertise our products.	根據總經理剛才的談話，我們部門將要進行產品宣傳工作。
B: We have tried lots of ways to change the situation. But it doesn't work. How can we carry on our advertising campaign?	我們已經嘗試了很多種方法來改善情況，但是都不能奏效。我們該如何進行我們的宣傳活動呢？
A: That's a good question. Considering these, I will ask you to carry out a market survey.	這是個好問題。考慮到以上的這些問題，我要妳們進行一次市場調查。
B: We will get right on it.	我們會馬上進行。
A: Good. Here are the questionnaires.	好。這些是調查問卷。

 關鍵單字要認得

speech *n.* 講話、言論	**The Queen gave an inspiring speech at the charity event.** → 女王在慈善活動發表了激勵人心的演說。
advertise our product *ph.* 宣傳產品	**We have to reconsider the strategy of how to advertise our product.** → 我們需要重新思考宣傳產品的策略。

try lots of ways to *ph.* 嘗試	**I have tried lots of ways to improved my grade.** → 我嘗試了許多不同方法提升學習成績。
situation *n.* 情況	**The situation is getting worse and worse.** → 情況變得越來越糟。
campaign *n.* 活動	**There's a campaign rally at the square.** → 廣場上有競選造勢活動。
considering these *ph.* 考慮到這些	**Considering these factors, we cancled our flight.** → 考量到這些因素，我們取消了我們原本訂的班機。

● ●

 一定要會的萬用句

① We have tried lots of ways to change the situation.
→ 我們已經嘗試了很多種方法來改善情況。

② How can we carry on our advertising campaign?
→ 我們該如何進行我們的宣傳活動呢？

③ That's a good question. → 這是個好問題。

④ We will get right on it. → 我們會馬上進行。

 我們也能這樣說

① The task will be completed on time. → 任務會按時完成。

② Let's speed things up. → 讓我們加快工作速度。

③ How's the project going? → 專案進行的如何？

④ We're right on target. → 我們在按照計畫進行。

⑤ We're running a little behind. → 我們進度慢了點。

常見錯誤不要犯

在英語片語中，介系詞有其固定的用法，如 "will ask you to carry away a market survey." 是不會使用的句子。

正確的說法是 "will ask you to carry out a market survey."

片語 carry away 意為「帶走、沖走、搬走、沖昏……的頭腦」；片語 carry out 意為「實行、執行、完成、實現」。從句子意思可知，市場調查應該要「執行、完成」。所以要用 carry out。

👍 **常見句型一起學**

★ 否定句

It   doesn't   work.
主詞　＋　don't / doesn't　＋　動詞原形

主詞＋don't / doesn't＋動詞原形，這個句型是一個否定句型。主詞除了 it 也可以是其他人稱代名詞或其他的事物。

以下是其他的相關例句：

▶ **The computer doesn't work.**
→ 電腦不能用了。

▶ **You don't know the fact.**
→ 你不知道真相。

▶ **She didn't come.**
→ 她沒來。

▶ **He doesn't go there.**
→ 他沒去那。

▶ **This plant doesn't grow.**
→ 這株植物不再生長了。

👍 **情境對話** 🎧 **Track 53**

會議結束時,都需要總結一下本次會議的討論結果與會議重點,方便相關同仁記錄與執行。

A: Now please allow me to draw a conclusion of this conference. We roughly know of our present situation. I hope I will get good news soon.	現在讓我對這場會議做個總結。我們對現況都大致瞭解。我希望不久就會有好消息傳來。
B: We will encourage our employees to work hard. And I do hope in our department there is no one lagging behind.	我們會鼓勵員工努力工作的。我也強烈希望在我們的部門中,人人都不甘落後。
A: That's right.	沒錯。
B: Our company is just like a big family. All of us belong to it.	我們的公司就像個大家庭一樣。我們都屬於這個大家庭。
A: OK, now let's call it a day!	好,今天就到此為止吧!

 關鍵單字要認得

draw a conclusion *ph.* 做出總結	**Can you draw a conclusion from the survey?** → 你可以從問卷調查總結出結論嗎?
conference *n.* 會議	**We'll discuss this later at the conference.** → 這件事情我們晚點會在會議中討論。

170

know of
ph. 瞭解

I know of the situation you're dealing with.
→ 我瞭解到了你們正面臨的狀況。

news
n. 消息

She always gets the first hand news.
→ 她總是掌握第一手消息。

encourage
v. 鼓勵

My parents always encourage me to try new things.
→ 我父母總是鼓勵我勇敢嘗試新事物。

 一定要會的萬用句

❶ Now please allow me to draw a conclusion to this conference.

→ 現在讓我對這場會議做個總結。

❷ I hope I will get good news soon.

→ 我希望不久就會有好消息傳來。

❸ Our company is just like a big family.

→ 我們的公司就像個大家庭一樣。

❹ Let's call it a day! → 今天就到此為止吧！

😎 我們也能這樣說

❶ We need to work hard these days.

→ 我們需要努力工作。

❷ I hope we can finish the task on time.

→ 我希望可以按時完成任務。

❸ We must encourage each other at work.

→ 我們在工作時，需要彼此鼓勵。

❹ This is our new target of this year. → 這是我們今年的新目標。

❺ Every department must do their best. → 每個部門都必須加油。

在英語文法中，特定詞彙有其固定的用法，如 "Now please allow me drawing a conclusion of this conference." 是不會使用的句子。

正確的說法是 "Now please allow me to draw a conclusion of this conference."

allow 作「允許」講，常搭用動詞不定式片語作受詞補語，即 allow sb. to do sth. 意為「允許某人做某事」；allow作「許可、允許」講，只可搭配動名詞片語作受詞，不可直接搭用動詞不定式作受詞補語，即只可說 allow doing sth.，不可說 allow sb. doing sth.。

👍 常見句型一起學

★ 強調 do 後面動詞的句型

I	do	hope	in our department there is no one lagging behind.
主詞 + do + 動詞原形 +			其他補語

這是一個強調句型，主要目的是用來強調 do 後面的動詞。do 根據主詞的不同可以有多種時態及單複數上的變化。句型意思是：「的確……、確實……」

以下是其他的相關例句：

▶ **I do hope you'll stay here a little longer.**
→ 我真希望你能在這裡多待一會兒。

▶ **I do know the fact.**
→ 我確實知道真相。

▶ **He does come.**
→ 他的確來了。

▶ **I did return this book.**
→ 我確實歸還這本書了。

▶ **We do expect you to do this.**
→ 我們真的很盼望你這麼做。

14 可以提供我相關資料嗎

在職場上經常會需要和同事，甚至是不同部門合力解決問題。需要協助，卻不知道要如何開口嗎？讓我們一起看看以下對話吧！

A: Hello, Mike. Sorry to bother you. Could you give me some information about the clients on my list?	你好，麥克。抱歉打擾了，你能提供我名單上客戶們的資訊嗎？
B: What for? I remember I gave the information to your department last week.	為什麼需要這份資料？我記得上個禮拜我已經給過你們部門了！
A: We lost some documents because there is something wrong with the computer. Hardly did I have enough time to response.	由於電腦出了點問題，有些檔案遺失了。我當時幾乎沒有足夠的時間反應。
B: I see. Luckily we have a backup copy.	我明白了。幸好我們有備份。
A: Thank God!	謝天謝地！
B: I'll give you later.	我稍後就給你。

 關鍵單字要認得

bother you *ph.* 打擾你	**May I bother you for a minute.** → 我可以打擾你一下嗎？
client *n.* 客戶	**This is a request from our client.** → 這是來自客戶的要求。

on my list *ph.* 在我的名單上	**I have quite a few fine dining restaurants on my list.** → 在我的口袋名單上有幾家高級餐廳。
document *n.* 文件	**Please send these documents to Mike.** → 麻煩你將這些文件寄給麥克。

• •

 一定要會的萬用句

❶ Sorry to bother you.

→ 抱歉打擾了。

❷ I gave the information to your department last week.

→ 上個禮拜我已經給過你們部門這份資料了！

❸ Lukily we have a backup copy.

→ 幸好我們有備份。

 我們也能這樣說

❶ Can you give me some files about the customers?

→ 你能給我一些有關這些顧客的文件嗎？

❷ Do you have a copy of this document?

→ 你有這份資料的副本嗎？

❸ Sorry to disturb you, may I ask some questions?

→ 打擾了，能問幾個問題嗎？

❹ Thank you for your help.　→ 謝謝你的幫忙！

❺ At last, we solved this problem together.

→ 終於，我們一起解決了這個問題。

常見錯誤不要犯

在英語中，有相似但字義有些微不同的單字，須視前後語意判斷用詞，如 "I'll give you latter." 是不會使用的句子。

正確的說法是 "I'll give you later."

latter 為形容詞，意為「後者的、近來的、後面的、較後的」；later 為副詞「後來、稍後、隨後」。再此句的末尾應該用的是副詞 later。兩個單字極為相似，但意義和用法都不同。注意區分。

常見句型一起學

★ 否定副詞放於句首的句型

Hardly did I have enough time to response.

Hardly + 助動詞 + 主詞 + 動詞

當否定副詞 hardly 放於句首時，後面的句子需要倒裝，使用動詞＋主詞的形式。這樣的結構適用於比較正式的場合。意思是「幾乎不……」。其中，hardly 還可以換成其他的否定副詞，如：never / seldom。

以下是其他的相關例句：

▶ **Hardly have I seen such a performance.**
→ 我幾乎都看不到如此好的表演了。

▷ **Hardly will you find her.**
→ 你是幾乎找不到她的。

▶ **Hardly do they have dinner together.**
→ 他們幾乎不在一起吃飯。

▷ **Hardly did the child fall asleep at night.**
→ 這個小孩晚上幾乎都不睡。

▶ **Hardly have I seen her in the classroom.**
→ 我幾乎沒看過她出現在教室。

15 你在這次案子表現突出

情境對話 🎧 Track 55

在工作上有亮眼的表現，是許多職員的願望。當受到上司讚賞時，我們可以怎麼回答呢？一起來看看吧！

A: I heard that you performed very well on this project.	我聽說你在這次的案子中表現突出。
B: It's my duty as an employee to carry it out. I received help from several departments while the whole matter was on the verge of failure.	這是我作為公司員工應盡的職責。在整件事情瀕臨失敗的情況下，我得到了許多部門的幫助。
A: Never give up, then we can defeat our rivals, no matter how strong they are. Good job!	永不放棄，我們才能打敗對手，不管他們多麼強大。你的表現很好！
B: Thanks for your praise. I'll keep working hard!	謝謝你的誇讚。我會繼續努力的！
A: Good.	很好。

關鍵單字要認得

perform	He performed greatly on his annual concert.
v. 表現	→ 他在年度演唱會上表現出色。
duty	It is my duty to protect the students.
n. 職責	→ 保護學生是我的職責。
carry it out	I couldn't have carried out the whole project if it wasn't for your help.
ph. 執行	→ 如果沒有你的幫助，我根本無法執行這個項目。

received help from	**I have received help from many people.**
_ph._ 從……得到幫助	→ 我從許多人那裡得到幫助。

on the verge of	**He was on the verge of tears when he heard the tragedy of his friend.**
_ph._ 瀕臨	→ 當他聽到友人的噩耗時，他瀕臨落淚。

rival	**Joker is Batman's biggest rival.**
_n._ 對手	→ 小丑是蝙蝠俠的最大勁敵。

praise	**Praise God!**
_n._ 讚美、誇讚	→ 讚美上帝！

• •

 一定要會的萬用句

❶ I heard that you performed very well on this project.

→ 我聽說你在這次的案子中表現突出。

❷ It's my duty as an employee to carry it out.

→ 這是我作為公司員工應盡的職責。

❸ Never give up, then we can defeat our rivals, no matter how strong they are. → 永不放棄，我們才能打敗對手，不管他們多麼強大。

❹ Thanks for your praise. → 謝謝你的誇讚。

 我們也能這樣說

① You look great today. → 你今天氣色很好。

❷ You surely did a good job! → 你的確表現得很好。

❸ We're very proud of you. → 我們十分為你驕傲。

❹ You have a very successful business. → 你的事業很成功。

⑤ I must say you're so professional. → 你真的很專業。

常見錯誤不要犯

要注意不定詞和動名詞的使用方法是否正確，如 "I'll keep to work hard!" 就是不會使用的句子。

正確的說法是 "I'll keep working hard!"

keep doing sth. 意為「保持不間斷地做某事」。keep doing sth. 還可表示連續不斷的動作或持續的狀態。keep 後面不能用動詞不定式。

常見句型一起學

★ 無論……多麼……

No matter　how　strong　they　are.

No matter　＋　how　＋　形容詞　＋　主詞　＋　be動詞／動詞

這個句型的意思是「無論……多麼……」的意思。how 後面一般接續形容詞來表示所修飾主詞的一種程度。

以下是其他的相關例句：

▶ **No matter how tough life was, she never complained about it.**
⟶ 不管生活如何艱苦，她從不抱怨。

▶ **You'll never succeed, no matter how hard you try.**
⟶ 無論你怎麼努力，你都不會成功的。

▶ **No matter how bad he is, he is still this old man's son.**
⟶ 不管他多壞，他仍是這個老人家的兒子。

▶ **I'll finish the job, no matter how long it takes.**
⟶ 不管花多少時間，我會完成這項工作。

▶ **No matter how cold it is, they keep on working.**
⟶ 無論天氣有多冷，他們仍繼續工作。

16 推銷系列產品的優惠活動

網路是現代社會行銷的利器，透過網路，可以更迅速推廣公司的優惠活動，也能拓展更多不同的客群。抓緊時間，學習處理相關事宜的英文會話吧！

A:	Have you informed HTM Co. that we are having a promotion for the HB series?	你有通知 HTM 公司我們現在 HB 系列有優惠嗎？
B:	Not yet, but I'm working on it now. I'm organizing a price list with pictures so that they can get all the information and specifications.	還沒，但我正在處理當中。我正在弄一張價目表並附上圖片，這樣他們就可以收到所有的資訊及產品規格。
A:	OK, that's a good idea. But please finish it ASAP. Time is passing quickly.	好，這個想法很好，但是你要盡快完成。時間很快就過去了喔。
B:	I will finish the price list and send it to HTM Co. by today.	我今天以前會完成價格表並寄給 HTM 公司。
A:	Good. Keep me posted.	很好，讓我知道最新狀況。
B:	Yes, I will.	是的！

關鍵單字要認得

promotion
n. 促銷活動

The company plans to have a promotion for new products.
→ 公司計畫要為了新產品辦促銷活動。

work on 🔳 執行；改善	**You need to work on your homework first.** → 你要先做回家作業。
pass 🔳 經過	**Days pass quickly. You are thirty years old now.** → 日子過得很快。你現在三十歲了。
send ... to 🔳 送某物到	**Please send the books to the school.** → 請把書寄到學校。

● ●

 一定要會的萬用句

❶ We are having a promotion for the HB series.

→ 我們現在 HB 系列有優惠。

❷ Not yet, but I'm working on it now. → 還沒，但我正在處理當中。

❸ Time is passing quickly. → 時間很快就過去了喔。

❹ Keep me posted. → 讓我知道最新狀況。

 我們也能這樣說

❶ This time we will offer a favorable discount to our customer.

→ 這次我們會給顧客提供優惠折扣。

❷ Have you decided to order some?

→ 你決定要訂購一些了嗎？

❸ Do you have any questions about our new products?

→ 你對我們的新產品有何問題嗎？

❹ I want a complete price list of your product.

→ 我想要一份你們產品完整的價格表。

❺ Let them know that we quote them the most favourable price.

→ 要讓他們知道我們報給他們的價格是最有競爭力的。

常見錯誤不要犯

要注意是否需要使用過去分詞，如 "Keep me post." 就是忘了要將動詞改成過去分詞。

正確的說法是 "Keep me posted."

Keep me posted. 意為「和我保持聯繫、有消息向我彙報」。是固定的表達方式。其中用的是 post 的過去分詞形式而不是原形。

常見句型一起學

★ 以便或以免

I'm organizing so that they can get all the information.

主句　　　　+　so that　+　　　　　　子句

主句＋so that＋子句，這個句型的意思是「……，以便或以免……」。

以下是其他的相關例句：

▶ **Unfold the map so that we can read it more easily.**
→ 把地圖攤開，以便閱讀。

▶ **He avoided candy so that he would not get fat.**
→ 他不吃糖果，以免讓自己變胖。

▶ **He closed the door softly so that he would not disturb anybody.**
→ 他關門很輕，以免打擾別人。

▶ **He got up early so that he could catch the first bus.**
→ 他早早就起床了，以便能趕上首班公車。

17 客戶希望重新報價

 情境對話　⌒ Track 57

報價的討論是商務往來中非常重要的環節，如果要向全球販售產品，網路是不可或缺的，在洽談交易時，一定要掌握相關的英語會話！

A: Sarah, bad news!	莎拉，壞消息！
B: What is it?	是什麼？
A: Mike thinks both our pricing and minimum order quantity are not satisfying. He needs to know if we can requote the price.	麥克說我們的報價和最低訂購量都不是很令他滿意。他想確認我們是不是可以重新報價。
B: If we could requote the price, could he accept all these terms?	如果我們重新報價，他能接受目前所有的條件嗎？
A: He didn't confirm, but he said he would try his best to convince his boss.	他尚未確認，但他說他會盡力說服他的老闆。
B: Okay, fair enough. Tell him we'll send out the revised pricing by today.	好，很合理。告訴他我們今天就會傳新的報價過去。
A: I see. And I'll update you as soon as possible.	知道了。一旦有任何最新消息，我會盡快向你報告。

 關鍵單字要認得

requote
☑ 重新報價

They don't accept the price we offered, so we have to requote the price.
→ 他們不接受我們提供的價格，我們必須重新報價。

accept all these terms

v/n 接受所有的條件

It's ridiculous! We can't accept all these terms.

→ 這太荒謬了！我們不能接受所有的條件。

confirm

v 確認

We have to call again to confirm the purchase order.

→ 我們要再打一次電話來確認訂單。

convince

v 說服

May convinced her boss to accept the price.

→ 梅說服她的老闆接受這個價錢。

一定要會的萬用句

① Mike thinks both our pricing and minimum order quantity are not satisfying. → 麥克說我們的報價和最低訂購量都不是很令他滿意。

② He said he would try his best to convince his boss.

→ 他說他會盡力說服他的老闆。

③ Fair enough. → 很合理。

我們也能這樣說

① Please confirm the purchase order so we can proceed with production. → 請確認這份訂單，我們才能開始生產。

② If you don't conform to our sales contract, we will end our business relationship with you.

→ 如果你不遵照合約的規定，我們將終止與你們生意上的往來。

③ Can you accept this price we offered today?

→ 你能接受我們今天提供的價格嗎？

④ Maybe we can have a discussion next week.

→ 也許我們下週可以討論一下。

⑤ That's the best price we could offer. → 這是我們能提供的最好價格了。

常見錯誤不要犯

不定詞的使用在英語中是相當重要的，要注意別用錯了，如
"But he said he would try his best convincing his boss." 就是
錯誤的說法。

正確的說法是 "But he said he would try his best to convince his boss."

這裡涉及 try 的用法。表達「盡某人最大的努力做某事」應用 try one's
best to do sth. 而不是 try one's best doing sth.。

常見句型一起學

★前後兩者都……

Both our pricing　and minimum order quantity　are not satisfying.

Both sth.　　+　　　　　and sth.　　　　　+　　其他補語

Both sth. and sth.＋其他補語的意思是「前後兩者都……」。

以下是其他的相關例句：

▶ **Both you and I are students.**
→ 你和我都是學生。

▷ **Both this point and that one are correct.**
→ 這個觀點和那個觀點都是正確的。

▶ **Both he and this boy will come to our party.**
→ 他和這個小男孩都會來參加派對。

▷ **Both this building and that building are our company's.**
→ 這兩棟樓都是我們公司的。

▶ **Both he and she are my friends.**
→ 他和她都是我的朋友。

情境對話 🎧 **Track 58**

在和全球做生意時，擁有一定的外語能力，學會相關的英語會話也是非常重要的。

A: Let's talk about the order.	我們來談談訂單的事吧。
B: Okay. What else do you want to add?	好的。你還需要什麼？
A: Our supplier insists on increasing MOQ to 1500 dozen or they would have problem processing your order.	我們的廠商堅持一定要將最低訂購量調到 1500 打，不然他們無法接你們的訂單。
B: That's a large order. We can't accept this.	這訂單數量太大了，我們無法接受。
A: Please understand we offer you the very best price. And we're willing to separate the whole batch into four shipments to benefit your company.	請瞭解我們給您的是最低的價格。而且，我們願意分四批出貨以利貴公司。
B: Hmm. Sounds fair. But I need to think it over. I'll let you know by this Friday.	嗯⋯⋯聽起來很合理。不過我還要再想一想，我禮拜五以前會告訴你答案。
A: I am looking forward to your favorable reply.	期待您的的好消息。

關鍵單字要認得

insist on
ph. 堅持

Harry insists on checking his homework twice.
→ 哈利堅持要檢查兩次作業。

process ... order	**We need the goods next month. Please process our order first.**
ph. 處理訂單	→ 我們下個月就要這批貨物。請先處理我們的訂單。
understand	**I don't understand your reason of standing me up.**
v. 明白	→ 我不能理解你放我鴿子的理由。
separate ... into ...	**John asked us to separate these books into two boxs.**
ph. 把……分成……	→ 約翰要求我們把這些書分別裝進兩個箱子。

. . . .

 一定要會的萬用句

1 What else do you want to add? → 你還想說什麼？

2 That's a large order. We can't accept this.

→ 這訂單數量太大了，我們無法接受。

3 Please understand we offer you the very best price.

→ 請瞭解我們給你的是最低的價格。

 我們也能這樣說

1 For large orders, we insist on payment by L/C.

→ 對於金額大的訂貨，我們要求開信用狀。

2 All right, if you insist, let's work on it.

→ 好吧，假如你堅持的話，我們就努力吧。

3 So sorry, you gave us a very large order which is beyond our capacity. → 對不起，你的訂單太大，超出我們能承受的範圍。

4 Can you rethink it, then dicide what to do?

→ 你能再想一下，然後決定如何做嗎？

5 We are looking forward to your reply. → 殷切盼望您的回覆。

常見錯誤不要犯

在英文中，介係詞是一個句子中很重要的存在，若是忽略介係詞就可能說出 "Our supplier insists in increasing MOQ to 1500 dozen." 的錯誤句子。

正確的說法是 "Our supplier insists on increasing MOQ to 1500 dozen."

片語 insist on 意為「堅持（做某事，認為）」，其中的介係詞是 on 而不是 in。另外，persist in 也是「堅持、固執於」的意思。這個片語中的介係詞才是 in。注意二者不能混用。

👍 常見句型一起學

★一般進行式

I   am   looking forward   to your favorable reply.

主詞 ＋ be 動詞 ＋   現在分詞   ＋   其他補語

主詞＋be 動詞＋動詞現在分詞＋其他補語，這是一個使用一般進行式的句型。be 動詞加上現在分詞，表達的意思是現在正在進行的動作。

以下是其他的相關例句：

▶ **I am reading my book.**
→ 我在看書。

▷ **He is talking with his friend.**
→ 他在和他的朋友交談。

▶ **She is looking for her cat.**
→ 她在找她的小貓。

▶ **My father is smoking.**
→ 我的爸爸在吸煙。

▶ **My teacher is looking at my papers.**
→ 我的老師正在看我的報告。

19 把訂單降價

 情境對話　∩ Track 59

在談訂單時，客戶多半會希望可以殺價，而是否能夠接受對方的價錢就需要請示主管，若能即時和主管溝通，就能省去談判需要耗費的時間。

A: What's the result about the order?	關於此次訂單有什麼結果了？
B: She will accept 1500 dozen on the condition that we lower the price to $12 per dozen.	她說如果我們把價格降至每打 12 美元，她就接受 1500 打的訂購量。
A: She's driving a hard bargain. How much per dozen now?	她真會殺價。目前一打是多少？
B: The current price is $16 per dozen.	目前是 16 美元一打。
A: What should we do?	你覺得我們應該怎麼做呢？
B: I think we should make it $12, she is one of our best customers.	我們應該降到 12 美元。畢竟她是我們最大的客戶之一。
A: OK. Make it to $12. The price is for her only.	好吧，降到 12 美元吧。這個價格只適用於她的訂單。

 關鍵單字要認得

lower the price *ph.* 降價	**Sam decided to lower the price to attract customers.** → 山姆決定要降價以吸引顧客。

drive a hard bargain _ph._ 很會殺價	**My mom is good at driving a hard bargain. We can buy goods at lower prices.** → 我媽媽很會殺價。我們可以用低價買到東西。
dozen _n._ 一打	**Please buy two dozen of eggs .** → 請買兩打雞蛋。
current _adj._ 目前的	**He is satisfied with his current life.** → 他很滿意現在的生活。

 一定要會的萬用句

❶ She will accept 1500 dozen on the condition that we lower the price to $12 per dozen.

→ 她說如果我們把價格降至每打 12 美元，她就接受 1500 打的訂購量。

❷ How much per dozen now? → 目前一打是多少？

❸ She is one of our best customers. → 她是我們最大的客戶之一。

❹ The price is for her only. → 這個價格只適用於她的訂單。

 我們也能這樣說

❶ Are you satisfied with our current price?

→ 您對我們現在的價格還滿意嗎？

❷ We still need a further discussion.

→ 我們還需要進一步討論。

❸ There is no discount at all. → 一點折扣都沒有。

❹ Can you reduce the price a little again?

→ 你能把價格再降低一點嗎？

❺ I don't accept the terms you put forward.

→ 我不能接受你們提出的條件。

189

在英文中，即使單字的意思相似也未必能通用，如 "The now price is $16 per dozen." 的錯誤句子。

正確的說法是 "The current price is $16 per dozen."

current 為形容詞，意為「現在的、當前的」。如果用 now 表達「當前的價格」則是：now the price 或者 the price now，不能說 the now price，沒有這種搭配。

常見句型一起學

★形容詞最高級

She   **is**   **one of our**   **best**   **customers.**

主詞 ＋ be動詞 ＋ one of ＋ 形容詞最高級 ＋ 名詞

主詞＋be＋one of＋形容詞最高級＋名詞，這個句型使用的是形容詞最高級。

以下是其他的相關例句：

▶ **Knife is one of the simplest tools.**
→ 刀是一種最普通的工具。

▶ **He is one of the most outstanding writers of the time.**
→ 他是當今最傑出的作家之一。

▶ **She is one of the best students in our class.**
→ 她是我們班最好的學生之一。

▶ **He is one of the greatest leader in the world.**
→ 他是世界上最偉大的領袖之一。

▶ **It is one of the most beautiful cars here.**
→ 這是這裡最漂亮的車之一。

20 訂單非常急

 情境對話　∩ Track 60

若對訂單有問題，或想提出要求，直接聯絡廠商是最迅速的事，要買到全世界的東西，就要學會相關英語會話！

A: May I ask you something?	我能問您一些事情嗎？
B: Of course!	當然可以了！
A: I'd like to know what your production lead time would be for a new order of 80K forks.	我想知道八萬支叉子從下單到出貨要多少時間。
B: We can provide 80K forks in one week.	我們一個星期就可以幫您出八萬支叉子的貨。
A: Can you ship earlier? This is very urgent. This order is for one of our customers.	能否更早出貨呢？這張訂單非常急，是我們的一個客戶下的。
B: Let me check the production schedule... I think we can make it within five days.	讓我查一下生產計畫表……我想我們可以五天內出貨給您。
A: That would be great! I will send you a new purchase order in no time.	那太好了！我會立刻寄新訂單過來給您。
B: Thank you. We will proceed with your order as soon as we receive it.	謝謝您。一收到您的訂單我們就會馬上處理。

 關鍵單字要認得

ship
☑ 船運；運送

We can ship the goods next Monday.
→ 我們可以下禮拜一出貨。

urgent *adj.* 緊急	**This order is urgent. We need to work on it now.** → 這份訂單很緊急。我們現在就要開始做。
schedule *n.* 行程表	**I will check my schedule after work.** → 我下班後會確認行程表。
within ... days *ph.* ……天內	**She will come back within two days.** → 她兩天內會回來。

- -

 一定要會的萬用句

1 I'd like to know what your production lead time would be for a new order of 80K forks.

→ 我想知道八萬支叉子從下單到出貨要多少時間。

2 I think we can make it within five days.

→ 我想我們可以五天內出貨給您。

3 I will send you a new purchase order in no time.

→ 我會立刻寄新訂單過來給您。

 我們也能這樣說

1 I want to change the date. → 我想更改日期。

2 I want to know whether I can get my goods three days in advance.

→ 我想知道我是否能提前三天收到貨。

3 Can you inform me if there is any change?

→ 如有變動，您能通知我嗎？

4 Let me consult our manager.

→ 請允許我問一下我們的經理。

5 I am afraid that we can't meet your needs.

→ 恐怕我們無法滿足你們的要求。

常見錯誤不要犯

在英文中，單字只差一個字母也是巨大的差別，如 "I will be sending you a new purchase order in not time." 就是錯誤的句子。

正確的說法是 "I will be sending you a new purchase order in no time."

片語 in no time 意為「立刻、很快、馬上」，相當於 at once / right away / immediately 等。是固定的搭配。用 no 而不是 not。

常見句型一起學

★一……就……

We will proceed with your order　as soon as　we receive it.

主句　　　　　　　　＋　as soon as　＋　　子句

主句＋as soon as＋子句，這個句型的意思是「一……就……」、「一……，馬上……」。

以下是其他的相關例句：

▶ **We solved problems as soon as they came up.**
→ 問題一出現我們就解決。

▶ **I will get there as soon as they do.**
→ 我會和他們同時到達那裡。

▶ **He fell asleep as soon as he lay down.**
→ 他一躺下就睡著了。

▶ **She will see you as soon as she can.**
→ 她一有空就會接見你。

▶ **My fahter left as soon as he heard the news.**
→ 我父親一聽到消息就離開了。

21 什麼時候可以收到貨款

 情境對話　∩ **Track 61**

若是交易有任何問題，最好都即時提出，透過網路在線上向對方提出疑問，或打電話詢問是最快的，若想催繳貨款最好直接向對方說明最為迅速，也更能釐清問題。

A: Sorry to bother you, but I want to know when we can receive your payment. It's a bit late since it's supposed to be made two months ago.	很抱歉打擾您，但是我想知道我們什麼時候可以收到您的貨款。這筆款項有點遲了，應該兩個月以前就要付了。
B: I'm sorry about the delay. We need another eight days to finish the procedures.	很抱歉延誤了。我們還需要八天來完成所有的手續。
A: Is it possible that you pay it earlier by the end of this month?	有沒有可能提早到這個月底以前付款呢？
B: The next payment run we're doing will be eight days later. This is when the invoice will be paid, not earlier. Please understand.	我們公司下一次的款項核發日是八天後。到那時才能付款，無法提早。請見諒。
A: Well, will you please pay us as soon as you finish all the procedures?	那麼請你一完成所有手續就付款給我們好嗎？
B: No problem.	沒問題。

 關鍵單字要認得

receive payment *ph.* 收到付款	**We should receive the payment this month.** → 我們這個月應該要收到貨款。

a bit late	**Getting home after eleven is a bit late.**
ph. 有點遲	→ 十一點過後回去有點晚。
delay	**The work should be done without delay.**
n. 延遲	→ 工作不能延遲。
possible	**It's not possible that coming back from America in a day.**
adj. 可能性	→ 一天內從美國回來是不可能的。

• •

 一定要會的萬用句

❶ I want to know when we can receive your payment.
→ 我想知道我們什麼時候可以收到您的貨款。

❷ We need another eight days to finish the procedures.
→ 我們還需要八天來完成所有的手續。

❸ Is it possible that you pay it earlier by the end of this month?
→ 有沒有可能提早到這個月底以前付款呢?

❹ This is when the Invoice will be paid, not earlier.
→ 到那時才能付款,無法提早。

 我們也能這樣說

❶ Can you wait another five days? → 你能再等五天嗎?

❷ Sorry, our payment is delayed several days.
→ 很抱歉,貨款延遲了幾天。

❸ Can you inform me if your company resumes normal services?
→ 假如你們公司恢復服務,可以通知我嗎?

❹ When can you finish these procedures?
→ 你們什麼時候可以完成這些手續?

❺ Thanks for your understanding for the delay.
→ 謝謝您諒解我們的延誤。

常見錯誤不要犯

在英文中，同一個單字可能有不同詞性，要避免擅自修改單字，如 "I'm sorry about the delayment." 是錯誤的用法。

正確的說法是 "I'm sorry about the delay."

此屬於單字的誤用。delay 本身既有動詞也有名詞「延期、耽擱」之意。所以 delay 無須再加-ment 來變為名詞。

常見句型一起學

★ 到那時……

This is when　　the invoice will be paid.

This is when　　　+　　　子句

This is when...這個句型的意思是「這就是……的時候」；「到那時……」。

以下是其他的相關例句：

▶ **This is when he will come.**
→ 這就是他要來的時候。

▶ **This is when you will be appointed.**
→ 這時，你就要被委派出去了。

▶ **This is when everyone is calm and thinks clearly.**
→ 此時，每個人頭腦冷靜、思路清晰。

▶ **This is when the product's features attract those potential buyers.**
→ 這時應該多強調產品的特色以吸引那些潛在買主。

▶ **This was when the two boys began to sing.**
→ 從那時起，兩個男孩就開始唱歌了。

22 你們必須換一批貨

 情境對話 ∩ **Track 62**

若是交易有任何問題，最好都即時提出，若想要求換貨，直接連絡對方的公司也是迅速的處理方式。

A: What do you want us to do?	您希望我們怎麼做呢？
B: You need to replace the spoons, or they'll inspect them and charge you back.	你們必須換一批湯匙，否則他們要整批檢查，然後向你們索賠。
A: I'm sorry for this. The replacement will be prepared and shipped by sea in four days.	對此我深感抱歉。四天內我們就會把替換的貨準備好並用海運寄出。
B: This is not acceptable. You got to air freight them.	這無法接受。你們必須空運寄出。
A: But the air freight would be too expensive to afford.	可是空運費太高我們負擔不起。
B: Airship the replacement, anyway. I'll ask them to share the cost.	無論如何還是用空運寄出。我會要求客戶分擔運費。
A: Thank you. We will proceed immediately.	謝謝你。我們會馬上進行。

 關鍵單字要認得

replace	**The laptop was broken, so we replaced it with a new one.**
☑ 更換	→ 筆電壞掉了，所以我們用新的來取代它。

prepare	Sam prepares dinner everyday .
v. 準備	→ 山姆每天都準備晚餐。

acceptable	All these terms are acceptable.
adj. 可接受的	→ 這些條件是可接受的。

share the cost	We will share the cost of the dinner.
ph. 分擔費用	→ 我們會分擔晚餐的費用。

* *

 一定要會的萬用句

❶ The replacement will be prepared and shipped by sea in four days.

→ 四天內我們就會把替換的貨準備好並用海運寄出。

❷ This is not acceptable. → 這無法接受。

❸ The air freight would be too expensive to afford.

→ 空運費太高我們負擔不起。

❹ I'll ask them to share the cost. → 我會要求他們分擔運費。

 我們也能這樣說

❶ I am so sorry for this. Please allow me to replace it.

→ 我對此深表歉意。請允許我為您替換產品。

❷ We'll deal with your problem right now.

→ 我們立刻就開始處理您的問題。

❸ We need the goods urgently. → 我們急需這批產品。

❹ We'll deliver the goods as soon as possible. → 我們會儘快送貨給你。

❺ If you receive it, please inform us immediately.

→ 如果你收到了，請立即通知我們。

常見錯誤不要犯

在英文中，即使單字的意思相似也未必能通用，如 "You need to exchange the spoons." 是錯誤的用法。

正確的說法是 "You need to replace the spoons."

exchange 是動詞「兌換、交易」的意思，也可以指文化方面的「交流」；replace 是動詞「取代、代替、替換、更換」的意思。貨物的更換應該用 replace 而不是 exchange。

常見句型一起學

★ 太……，以至於不能……

The air freight　would be　too　expensive　to　afford.
　　主詞　　　　　+　　be動詞　　+ too +　　形容詞　　+ to +　動詞

主詞＋be動詞＋too＋形容詞＋to＋動詞，這個句型的意思是「太……了，以至於不能……」。中間用的是形容詞原形。

以下是其他的相關例句：

▶ **This watch is too expensive to buy.**
→ 這手錶貴得買不起。

▷ **It's too late to help him.**
→ 太遲了，無法幫他了。

▶ **He was too lazy to work.**
→ 他懶於工作。

▷ **They seemed to be too anxious to leave.**
→ 他們看來太過急於離開。

▶ **It's too eary to say that.**
→ 現在下定論還太早。

23 年度銷售成績必須提升

 情境對話　∩ Track 63

一間公司在發展時，一定會定期檢視公司業績，檢討公司的效能，訂立未來的目標，這些都是很重要的。

A: Let's start our meeting now. Please keep track of today's meeting.	會議開始吧！麻煩做會議記錄。
B: OK. And I will post the meeting minutes on the internet as well.	好的。我也會把會議記錄張貼在網路上。
A: Thank you. You're very thoughtful. Let's get into the subject now. This year's sales must be raised.	謝謝，妳考慮很周全。我們進入正題吧！本年度的銷售成績必須提升。
B: How do you achieve the goal?	你要怎麼提升？
A: In the following months, I expect each of you to have at least five new clients every month.	接下來的幾個月裡，我希望大家每個月務必開發至少五名客戶。
B: We will try our best to achieve the goal!	我們會盡最大的努力達成目標！
A: Great. Come on, everybody!	很好。大家都加油！

 關鍵單字要認得

meeting minutes
ph. 會議記錄

Can you take the meeting minutes?
→ 請問你可以做會議紀錄嗎？

200

as well

ph. 也

Sam likes horror movies and fantasy movies as well.
→ 山姆喜歡恐怖電影和奇幻電影。

thoughtful

adj. 考慮周到的

It's thoughtful that you brought drinks for us.
→ 你帶飲料來給我們是考慮得很周到的。

subject

n. 主題

Let's start our subject.
→ 我們進入主題吧。

- -

 一定要會的萬用句

❶ Please keep track of today's meeting. → 麻煩做會議紀錄。

❷ I will post the meeting minutes on the internet as well.

→ 我也會把會議紀錄張貼在網路上。

❸ This year's sales must be raised. → 本年度的銷售成績必須提升。

❹ We will try our best to achieve the goal!

→ 我們會盡最大的努力達成目標！

 我們也能這樣說

❶ Please stick the poster on the wall. → 請把這張海報貼在牆上。

❷ You can paste something cute on the paper.

→ 你可以在紙上貼些可愛的東西。

❸ How do you know he is the right person?

→ 你怎麼知道他就是對的人選？

❹ I will try my best to keep the client!

→ 我會盡力留住那個客戶！

❺ She always posts photos on her blog.

→ 她總在她的部落格上張貼照片。

常見句型一起學

★ 怎麼、如何

How   do   you   achieve the goal?

How ＋ 助動詞 ＋ 主詞 ＋ 　　　動詞／ to do

How to achieve the goal? 也可以省略為How? 作為單獨的句子。另外，當 how 置於句首，用來詢問「怎麼、如何」時，後面不能接 to。how 除了可單獨形成一個疑問句，還可用於以下問句：

▶ **How do you know Janice from the Human Resource Department?**

→ 你怎麼會認識人事部的珍妮絲？

若要在陳述句裡表示「知道怎麼」，就能用 how to：

▶ **He doesn't know how to operate that machine.**

→ 他不知道該怎麼操作這台機器。

24 檢討團隊績效

情境對話　∩ Track 64

主管應該要定期檢視團隊的工作情況，檢討團隊的績效。要瞭解這些不必限於請整個部門來開會，也可以藉由網路在線上開會。

A: How is everything going? What has your team been doing lately?	一切還順利嗎？你的部門最近在做些什麼？
B: So far so good. At least our department isn't falling apart. We have a progress meeting at four every Friday.	到目前為止，一切順利。至少我們部門沒有四分五裂。我們每週五的四點會開進度會議。
A: So do you think it works?	你覺得有效嗎？
B: I have no doubt! It is necessary for us to review our results week by week. I get to keep track of each person's results.	當然有效！我認為每週檢討成績是必要的。這樣我才得以追蹤每個人的表現。
A: You made a very intelligent decision. What about the team members?	你的決策很明智。那組員的情況如何？
B: I'm trying my best to smooth the way for them. I am looking forward to seeing a lively and successful team. Not to mention, excellent results as well.	我盡力幫助他們解決問題。我期待看到一個朝氣蓬勃、成功的團隊。當然，還有亮眼的成績。

 關鍵單字要認得

no doubt

ph. 無疑

There is no doubt that he is the best client ever.
→ 他毫無疑問是有史以來最棒的客戶。

necessary *adj.* 必要的	**Every employee is necessary for the company.** → 每個員工對公司來說都是必要的。
keep track of *ph.* 記錄、追蹤	**We will keep track of your progress.** → 我們會追蹤你的進度。
intelligent *adj.* 明智的	**It's an intelligent decision.** → 這是一個明智的決定。
smooth *v.* 使順利	**Parents always try to smooth their children's way.** → 父母總是試著為他們小孩建立一條康莊大道。

• •

 一定要會的萬用句

❶ What has your team been doing lately? → 你的部門最近在做些什麼？

❷ It is necessary for us to review our results week by week.
→ 我認為每週檢討成績是必要的。

❸ I get to keep track of each person's results.
→ 這樣我才得以追蹤每個人的表現。

❹ I'm trying my best to smooth the way for them.
→ 我盡力幫助他們解決問題。

 我們也能這樣說

❶ I shall see you at ten Monday morning. → 我週一早上十點見你。

❷ The auction will be started at six on Saturday night.
→ 拍賣會將在週六晚上六點開始。

❸ It is necessary for us to hold a welcome party for our chairman.
→ 我們有必要為主席舉行一場歡迎會。

❹ It is necessary for the people to fight over justice.
→ 人們有必要爭取正義。

❺ The team was falling apart. → 那個團隊四分五裂了。

常見錯誤不要犯

在英文中，即使單字的意思相似，也未必能夠通用，如 "So far very good." 就是錯誤的。

正確的說法是 "So far so good."

So far so good. 是「到目前為止還好」的意思。是個固定的表達方式。不可隨意替換裡面的每一個字。

常見句型一起學

★ 有必要做某事

It is necessary for us to review our results week by week.

It is necessary + for + 名詞 + to do + 其他

這個句型是用來表達有必要做某事。

以下是其他的相關例句：

▶ **It is necessary for me to think it over.**
→ 我有必要考慮一下。

▶ **It is necessary not to change.**
→ 不做任何改變是必要的。

25 我很滿意你的能力

在工作上得到成就感是很重要的一環，尤其是在簽下一份大合約之後更是如此。若身為主管，應該即時鼓勵員工，藉此讓員工在未來繼續和公司一起努力。

A: I've got something to tell you. I just came back from Sunrise Limited, and they decided to sign a one-year contract with us.	我有話要跟你說。我剛拜訪完日出有限公司，他們同意和我們簽一年的合約。
B: Excellent! I told you so. Where there's a will, there's a way.	太好了！我就說吧，有志者事竟成。
A: Yes. I'm glad that I listened to your advice.	沒錯。當初聽你的忠告是對的。
B: I'm pleased with your ability.	對於你的能力，我感到很滿意。
A: Thank you. I will keep working hard!	謝謝你。我會繼續努力的！
B: Great!	很好！

 關鍵單字要認得

come back from *ph.* 從……回來	**Sam came back from America.** → 山姆從美國回來。
contract *n.* 合約	**We will begin to work after signing the contract.** → 簽訂合約後，我們會開始工作。

advice
n. 建議、忠告

I will take your advice on which book to buy.
→ 在買哪一本書的問題上，我會採用你的建議。

be pleased with
ph. 對……感到滿意

He's pleased with his new computer.
→ 他很滿意他的新電腦。

ability
n. 能力

John has the ability to know what other people really think.
→ 約翰有能力知道其他人在想什麼。

- -

 一定要會的萬用句

❶ I've got something to tell you. → 我有話要跟你說。

❷ They decided to sign a one-year contract with us.

　　→ 他們同意和我們簽一年的合約。

❸ Where there's a will, there's a way. → 有志者事竟成。

❹ I'm pleased with your ability. → 對於你的能力，我感到很滿意。

 我們也能這樣說

❶ I don't need advice from a loser. → 我不需要失敗者給予的建議。

❷ They don't know the reason why you were late.

　　→ 他們不知道你們遲到的原因。

❸ You should have a three-month probation.

　　→ 你應該有三個月的試用期。

❹ I just came back from the office. → 我剛從辦公室回來。

❺ He doesn't understand what the policeman is questioning about.

　　→ 他不明白員警正在問什麼。

常見錯誤不要犯

介係詞在英文中是非常重要的，用錯介係詞會使整個句子出錯，如 "I'm pleased for your ability." 就是錯誤的。

正確的說法是 "I'm pleased with your ability."

片語 be pleased with sth. / sb. 意為「對某物／某人感到滿意」。這是固定的搭配，其中的介係詞應該是 with 而不是 for。

 常見句型一起學

★ 表達「如果」

Where there's a will, there's a way.

Where 條件句   +   主句

表達「如果」除了常用的 if 之外，where 也可以引導條件句，如要表達「有愛就有希望」可以說 If there's love, there's hope. 或者可以說 Where there's love, there's hope.

以下是其他的相關例句：

▶ **Where there's effort, there's success.**
→ 只要努力就會成功。

▷ **Where there's a start, we should keep on.**
→ 只要開始了，就要繼續下去。

▶ **If there's strong will, we will overcome all difficulties.**
→ 只要意志堅定，我們就能克服一切困難。

▷ **If there's confidence, we'll make it.**
→ 只要有信心，我們就能成功。

▶ **Where there's courage, there's a hero.**
→ 有勇氣就能成為英雄。

26 相信你一定會成功

工作常常讓人感到疲憊，在發覺同事的狀況不好的時候，可以分他一點小點心鼓勵他，若是雙方沒有在同一個工作地點，而是在線上開會的話，也可以多說一些鼓勵的話。

A: You look tired. How is everything going?	你看起來很累。工作進行得如何？
B: As usual, I keep visiting clients, working on proposals and making phone calls.	老樣子，不停地拜訪客戶、寫提案和打電話。
A: Most people think that the work can be tiresome and they start to lose interest.	大多數的人認為這種工作很煩人，所以就失去興趣了。
B: I agree with you. Sometimes the clients' refusals cause me great distress.	我同意。有時候客戶拒絕也讓我感到非常痛苦。
A: Come on! I believe you can make it.	加油！我相信你一定會成功的。

關鍵單字要認得

as usual _ph._ 像往常一樣	**As usual, he arrived in the office at nine o'clock sharp.** → 他像往常一樣九點準時到辦公室。
client _n._ 客戶	**The client accepted all these terms.** → 客戶接受所有的條件。

agree with	**Our boss didn't agree with what you said.**
ph. 同意	→ 我們的老闆不同意你說的話。

refusal	**Her refusal was very clear.**
n. 拒絕	→ 她的拒絕非常清楚。

- -

 一定要會的萬用句

❶ As usual, I keep visiting clients, working on proposals and making phone calls.

→ 老樣子，不停地拜訪客戶、寫提案和打電話。

❷ Most people think that the work can be tiresome and they start to lose interest.

→ 大多數的人認為這種工作很煩人，所以就失去興趣了。

❸ Sometimes the clients' refusals cause me great distress.

→ 有時候客戶拒絕也讓我感到非常痛苦。

 我們也能這樣說

❶ A long vacation is exactly what I need.

→ 我正好需要放長假。

❷ He found it hard to live an ordinary life.

→ 他發現很難去過平凡的生活。

❸ You are exactly the one I need.

→ 你正是我所需要的人。

❹ Would you like to have some snacks?

→ 你要吃點零食嗎？

❺ I am glad to see your achievement.

→ 很高興看到你的成就。

常見錯誤不要犯

過去分詞和現在分詞的使用容易搞混，要避免犯下如 "You look tiring." 的錯誤。

正確的說法是 "You look tired."

現在分詞 tiring 的意思是「累人的、麻煩的、無聊的、引起疲勞的」；
過去分詞 tired 的意思是「疲倦的、厭倦的、厭煩的」。二者的區別是：tiring 是某物令人疲憊；而 tired 是某人感到疲憊。

常見句型一起學

★ 某事引起某人如何

The clients' refusals　　　cause me great distress.

sth.　　　　　　　　　+　　　　　　cause sb. sth.

這個句型的意思是「某事引起某人如何」。

以下是其他的相關例句：

▶ **That causes me to think deeply.**
→ 這不禁讓我深思起來。

▷ **It causes him to go farther.**
→ 這讓他走了不少遠路。

▶ **The notice caused me to feel angry.**
→ 這個通知讓我感到很生氣。

▷ **His words caused me to feel sad.**
→ 他的話語讓我感到傷心。

▶ **It causes me to rethink that deicision.**
→ 這不禁讓我重新思考那個決定。

27 假期結束了

 情境對話　∩ Track 67

對員工來說，能好好享受一個假期是非常快樂的，而假期的結束也讓人感到格外悲傷。在假期即將結束之際，免不了想找人抒發，這樣的心情也可以用英文來表達喔！

A: How time flies! The vacation has come to an end. If only the vacation could be longer, I would be overjoyed.	時間過得真快啊！假期就要結束了。要是假期能再久一點，我就會高興得不得了。
B: Day dreaming again! There is a lot of work for us to do back in the office. The longer the vacation is, the more work we have to do.	又在做白日夢了！公司裡還有好多工作等著我們完成。假期越久，要做的事情越多。
A: So it is! Your judgment has matured faster than I thought it would. Good!	是啊！你的判斷力成熟得比我想像的要快得多。這樣很好啊！
B: The only thing that upsets me is I have to get up before seven. Oh, my God!	唯一讓我沮喪的是要在七點前起床。啊，我的老天啊！
A: I feel the same way!	我也是！

 關鍵單字要認得

time flies
ph. 時光飛逝

Time flies when we are busy.
→ 我們在忙的時候時間過得很快。

vacation *n.* 假期	**I went to Japan on vacation.** → 我利用假期去日本。
come to an end *ph.* 結束	**This trip has come to an end.** → 旅程就要結束了。
mature *v.* 成熟	**He matured a lot after graduation.** → 畢業之後他變得很成熟。

• •

 一定要會的萬用句

❶ Day dreaming again!

→ 又在做白日夢了！

❷ There is a lot of work for us to do back in the offlce.

→ 公司裡還有好多工作等著我們完成。

❸ Your judgment has matured faster than I thought it would.

→ 你的判斷力成熟得比我想像的要快得多。

 我們也能這樣說

❶ What a wonderful holiday!

→ 這假期真棒！

❷ Have you already got the ticket?

→ 你已經拿到票了嗎？

❸ When will we leave here?

→ 我們什麼時候離開這裡？

❹ Have you put all the clothes in your suitcase?

→ 你把所有的衣服都放行李箱了嗎？

常見錯誤不要犯

在英文中，即使單字的意思都對了，但文法錯誤的話就仍是錯誤的句子，如 "How time past!" 就是錯誤的。

正確的說法是 "How time flies!"

past 是形容詞「過去的、結束的」的意思。雖然在中文意思上看起來似乎是符合的，但是就英文文法來講，how time 後面要接的應該是動詞，否則就不能成為一個完整的句子。

 常見句型一起學

★ 越……，就越……

The longer we stay here, the more we have to do.

The + 比較級 + 主詞 + 動詞 + the + 比較級 + 主詞 + 動詞

這個句型的意思是「越……，就越……。」前後之間有因果關係的意味，因為前面情況的發生，而連帶出現了後面的情況。

以下是其他的相關例句：

▶ **The more you learn, the more you know.**
→ 你學得越多，知道的也就越多。

▷ **The harder you work, the more you earn.**
→ 你越努力工作，賺的也越多。

▶ **The harder you study, the more progress you make.**
→ 你越認真唸書，你就越進步。

▷ **The more you get, the more you want.**
→ 得到的越多，想要的也越多。

▶ **The more you do, the greater you are.**
→ 你做得越多，越偉大。

28 你能幫我一個忙嗎

 情境對話　🎧 Track 68

即使是有經驗的員工，也可能會在工作時犯錯，而職場菜鳥則更需要幫助。若是身邊剛好沒有同事可以幫忙，就會需要線上求助了。

A: Could you do me a favor?	你能幫我一個忙嗎？
B: Sure, what's wrong?	當然。怎麼了？
A: There is a serious error in my documents. Tom told me you have rich experience in verifying data, so...	我的檔案出現了一個嚴重的錯誤。湯姆告訴我，你在審核資料這方面經驗相當豐富，所以……
B: I think what you need Is the documents of 1999, I am afraid you have to ask the accounting department for help.	我覺得目前你所需要的是 1999 年的資料。恐怕你得請會計部幫忙了。
A: I see. Thanks a lot!	我明白了。非常感謝！
B: You are welcome.	不客氣。

 關鍵單字要認得

do me a favor *ph.* 幫我一個忙	**I need someone to do me a favor.** → 我需要有人幫我個忙。
error *n.* 錯誤	**There are some typing errors in the message.** → 信裡有一些打字上的錯誤。

| **ask ... for help**
ph. 請……幫忙 | **Sarah forgot to do her homework, so she asked me for help.**
→ 莎拉忘記做她的作業，所以她請我幫忙。 |
| **accounting dapartment**
n. 會計部 | **The accounting department keeps records of the payment we received.**
→ 會計部會記錄我們收到的款項。 |

● ●

 一定要會的萬用句

❶ Could you do me a favor? → 你能幫我一個忙嗎？

❷ There is a serious error in my documents.

→ 我的檔案出現了一個嚴重的錯誤。

❸ Tom told me you have rich experience in verifying data.

→ 湯姆告訴我，你在審核資料這方面經驗相當豐富。

❹ I am afraid you have to ask the accounting department for help.

→ 恐怕你得請會計部幫忙了。

 我們也能這樣說

❶ Can you give me a hand? → 您能幫我一下嗎？

❷ Can you point out my mistakes in the papers?

→ 你能幫我看看這些文件裡哪裡有錯誤嗎？

❸ I'd better ask our manager for help.

→ 我最好向經理求助一下。

❹ I need some important files to complete this project.

→ 我需要一些很重要的檔案才能完成這個專案。

❺ I must go to the archive to find out some old documents.

→ 我必須去檔案室找一些舊檔案。

常見錯誤不要犯

在英文中，會有不同片語表達同一個意思的情況，可能會造成混淆，要注意不要犯下如 "Could you do me a hand?" 的錯誤。

正確的說法是 "Could you do me a favor?"

表達「幫忙」的片語有：give a hand 和 do a favor，這些都是固定的表達方式。不能說 do a hand 或者 give a favor。兩者間不能互相混淆。

常見句型一起學

★ 某人告訴某人某事

Tom	**told**	**me**	**you have rich experience in...**
主詞 +	tell +	受詞 +	that 子句

這個句型的意思是某人告訴某人某事。that 引導告知的具體內容，that 可省略。

以下是其他的相關例句：

▶ **Would you tell Tom that I called?**
→ 你能告訴湯姆我打了電話給他嗎？

▶ **He hasn't told anyone about it.**
→ 他還沒告訴任何人。

▶ **Would you tell me your decision?**
→ 你願意告訴我你的決定嗎？

▶ **He told me that you came here.**
→ 他告訴我說你到這裡來了。

▶ **I was told that you were ill.**
→ 我被告知你生病了。

29 尋求協助

若是需要幫助時，身邊剛好沒有同事可以幫忙，可以嘗試線上求助。在需要跟對方說明遇到的問題的時候，也可以輔以照片或圖像喔。

A: Are you busy right now?	你現在忙嗎？
B: Not really. What's up?	不至於啦。怎麼了嗎？
A: Well, I need a hand with the fax machine. My fax is not going through.	嗯，我需要有人幫我處理傳真機。我無法將文件傳過去。
B: I'm kind of useless in that area, but I'll take a look at it.	我在這方面不太行，但是我可以幫你看一下。
A: Thanks a bunch! I'll send you the photo of the fax machine.	多謝！我會把傳真機的照片傳給你。
B: It looks like you forget the area code.	看起來像是你沒有撥區域號碼。
A: Ha! I am so stupid! Thank you!	哈！我太笨了！謝謝你！

 關鍵單字要認得

fax *n.* 傳真	**Please send me a fax with the details.** → 請把細節傳真給我。
kind of *ph.* 稍微、有點	**I feel kind of sorry for him because of the refusal.** → 我對拒絕他感到有點抱歉。

take a look
ph. 看一看

Can you take a look at the book?
→ 你可以看一下這本書嗎？

look like
ph. 看起來像

It looks like they are going home.
→ 看起來他們好像是要回家了。

 一定要會的萬用句

❶ Not really. → 不至於啦。

❷ My fax is not going through.

→ 我無法將文件傳真過去。

❸ I'm kind of useless in that area.

→ 我在這方面不太行。

❹ Thanks a bunch! → 多謝！

 我們也能這樣說

❶ There's a problem with my fax machine.

→ 我的傳真機有問題。

❷ It's still not working. → 它還是沒有運轉。

❸ I'd better ask our manager for help.

→ 我最好向經理求助一下。

❹ Let's go through the issue again.

→ 讓我們再來討論一下這個問題。

❺ They went through with the party.

→ 他們舉行了宴會。

❻ I know nothing about it. Perhaps you need to find another helper.

→ 我對此一無所知，你或許得找別人幫忙。

在英文中，會有不同片語表達同一個意思的情況，可能會造成混淆，要注意不要犯下如 "I'm a kind of useless in that area." 的錯誤。

正確的說法是 "I'm kind of useless in that area."

片語 a kind of 意為「一種、一類、一樣」；片語 kind of 意為「稍微、有點兒、有幾分」，也可以說 sort of。兩者意思不同，注意區分。

👍 常見句型一起學

★ 怎麼了

What　is　up?

What　+ be動詞 + 介詞／形容詞

問「怎麼了？」、「發生了什麼事？」可以說 What's up? 也可以說 What's wrong?

以下是其他的相關例句：

▶ **What happened?**
→ 發生什麼事了？

▶ **What happened to him?**
→ 他出了什麼事了？

▶ **What's the matter?**
→ 怎麼了？

▶ **What's the problem?**
→ 有什麼問題？

▶ **What gives?**
→ 出了什麼事？

30 約訪客戶

當雙方需要開會，卻抽不出時間見面時，就可以改為開線上會議，讓時間安排更有彈性。

A: Hello, Bruce. How's everything?	喂，布魯斯，你好嗎？
B: Can't complain. How about you?	很好。你呢？
A: Business is booming. I understand there will be a meeting next week. How's your schedule looking?	生意很好。我知道下週有個會議。你何時方便呢？
B: Let me see.... I'm out of town from Monday to Wednesday. Can we have the meeting online on Wednesday?	讓我想想……我星期一到星期三外出。我們可以星期三線上開會嗎？
A: Great. Shall I pencil you in for Wednesday morning at 9:30?	太棒了。那我先跟你約週三早上，九點半好嗎？
B: 9:30 is fine.	九點半沒問題。
A: OK. See you then.	好的。那到時候見囉。

 關鍵單字要認得

complain ☑ 抱怨	**He complained about work.** → 他抱怨工作。
boom ☑ 興旺	**Our company is booming.** → 我們的公司蓬勃發展。

221

| **out of town**
 ph. 外出 | **I wiil be out of town next Sunday.**
 → 我下禮拜天會外出。 |
| **pencil ... in**
 ph. 臨時安排；草定 | **Can you pencil me in for the trip?**
 → 你可以先安排我一起旅行嗎？ |

- -

 一定要會的萬用句

❶ Can't complain. → 很好。

❷ Business is booming. → 生意很好。

❸ I'm out of town from Monday to Wednesday.

→ 我星期一到星期三外出。

❹ Shall I pencil you in for Wednesday morning at 9:30?

→ 那我先跟你約週三早上，九點半好嗎？

😎 **我們也能這樣說**

❶ My company just made a fat profit.

→ 我的公司才剛大賺了一筆。

❷ Business went down.

→ 生意下滑。

❸ The sales dropped during the first quarter.

→ 第一季的營業額下降。

❹ What's your schedule like?

→ 你的行程如何呢？

❺ When is the best time for you to meet up?

→ 何時方便見面呢？

常見錯誤不要犯

中文和英文大不相同，不能直接中翻英，如 "Can't say bad." 就是錯誤的。

正確的說法是 "Can't complain."

can't complain 意為「很好、不會抱怨、好得沒話說」。這種表達日常口語中常用。説自己近況不錯，不僅可以説 very good, very well 等，還可以靈活運用些其他的表達方式。

常見句型一起學

★ **您何時方便呢**

How　is　your schedule　looking?

How　＋　be 動詞　＋　名詞　　＋　其他

How's your schedule looking? 這句話的意思是「您何時方便呢？」，是在問對方何時有空。詢問對方情況如何時會用到類似的句子，如 How are you doing recently?（你最近怎麼樣啊？）

以下是其他的相關例句：

▶ **How's another flight?**
→ 另一航班呢？

▶ **How's everything going?**
→ 一切都好嗎？

▶ **How's he doing?**
→ 他怎麼樣？

▶ **How's it going?**
→ 日子過得怎樣？

▶ **How's business?**
→ 生意怎麼樣？

原來如此 系列 *E272*

外商我來了！
必學實用英語會話，一本通通搞定！

70篇精選會話╳關鍵文法句型，揪出常見文法錯誤，為加入外商打好底子！

作　　　者	許澄瑄
顧　　　問	曾文旭
社　　　長	王毓芳
編輯統籌	耿文國、黃璽宇
主　　　編	吳靜宜
執行主編	潘妍潔
美術編輯	王桂芳、張嘉容
法律顧問	北辰著作權事務所　蕭雄淋律師、幸秋妙律師

初　　　版	2024年5月
出　　　版	捷徑文化出版事業有限公司
電　　　話	（02）2752-5618
傳　　　真	（02）2752-5619

定　　　價	新台幣350元／港幣117元
產品內容	1書

總 經 銷	采舍國際有限公司
地　　　址	235新北市中和區中山路二段366巷10號3樓
電　　　話	（02）8245-8786
傳　　　真	（02）8245-8718

港澳地區總經銷	和平圖書有限公司
地　　　址	香港柴灣嘉業街12號百樂門大廈17樓
電　　　話	（852）2804-6687
傳　　　真	（852）2804-6409

▶本書部分圖片由Shutterstock、freepik提供

捷徑 Book站